Body at the Bakery

A Cornish Witch Mystery

Stella Berry

If you would like to be informed immediately when future books by this author are released then visit the website www.stellaberrybooks.com

This book was written and edited in the UK, where some spelling, grammar and word usage will vary from US English

Dedicated to some fabulous cozy mystery writers:

Bella Falls and Elle Adams for encouraging me to continue as we took high tea in Bath. Annabel Chase for telling me to drink the cool-aid. Ellie Moses for making it way better, and Amanda M Lee, because NINC, baby! (Imagine me saying that in Vince Vaughn's voice, otherwise it's weird, lol).

Contents

Prologue

Kendra pulled the comb out of her hair and dropped it on her dressing table with a depressed sigh. All that effort wasted, all that money spent on her clothes and her hair and her nails, and he hadn't even commented on how good she looked. Not that the expense mattered now, but she'd been so sure it would pay itself back in spades.

She slumped onto her bed, her fingers burying themselves in the thick fur of her new throw. Gregory was supposed to be making love to her on top of this throw right now, not heading back to his hotel alone.

Surely he wasn't just going to leave it like that?

She lifted her phone to her face to check it even though she knew it hadn't made a sound and wished she could call her best friend. She needed some reassurance, and to hear that she hadn't been too cool or too clingy. Except she didn't have a best friend now. She had no one. Everyone left her and moved on with their lives. She thought her inheritance would change everything but instead it had alienated her even more.

She decided it was just as well that there was no one to call because Gregory might ring at any moment to say he'd changed his mind. She half expected it, honestly. He'd be on the street outside arguing with his conscience right now, but temptation would get the better of him. Wouldn't it?

A brief but firm knock rattled the door of her

apartment. She jumped to her feet, moving out of the bedroom with a knowing smile across her face.

Kendra looked through the peephole to check that it wasn't some random stranger then threw open the door and flung her arms around the man standing there.

In her final moments, his betrayal hit her hard. He'd come back just when she thought she had no one, but he was cold and emotionless now.

The rope at her neck tightened and she thought nothing more.

Chapter One

The sea was red.

Of course, the dawn sky was red too so perhaps it wasn't surprising.

"But as signs go it's not good," Morgana commented aloud even though she was alone.

She waited, staring out at the water until the May Day morning sunshine crested the cliffs and hit her in all its brilliant glory. She gave a sigh of satisfaction as the sea below turned a vibrant blue. The birds came out from their nests in the cliff and began to circle and call like noisy children and the feeling of bad omens was broken.

She yawned widely and got to her feet. "Time to head back. Can't sit staring at the water like a tourist all day."

Ten minutes later, Morgana licked a stray dollop of jam off the back of her hand before returning with gusto to the Cornish Cream Tea in front of her. Freshly made scones, still warm from the oven, with thick clotted cream and her sister's own strawberry jam.

Apply cream and jam liberally and devour, Morgana thought, spreading the clotted cream thickly onto the second half of the scone.

"So, what's the verdict?" Opposite Morgana, Ellie tilted her head questioningly as she watched her younger sister try out the new batch of jam.

"Ish good," Morgana said through a mouthful of scone.

"Yes, but is it as good as last years? The strawberries have had more sun this year but less rain. They're bigger, but maybe not as juicy?" Ellie twisted the tea towel in her hands clearly perturbed by the lack of decisive judgement she was getting.

Ellie was plump and motherly with her hair secured in a bun on the back of her head, and her easy smile and round cheeks made her look the epitome of a Cornish café owner. There was no visible sign at all that she was also a witch, and unlike Morgana, she did nothing to allude to it either.

Morgana dabbed her mouth with a paper napkin and smiled. "Don't fret. Your jam gets better every single year without fail. It's a triumph and perfectly juicy."

Ellie heaved out a relieved sigh. "You're not just saying that? Of course, these are just the early variety strawberries. The best jamming ones won't be fully ripe until June, but these are a good indication of how the rest of the season will taste."

"The season tastes heavenly," Morgana assured her. "Business will be booming as usual." She looked around the warm bakery-come-tearoom-come-jam store that her sister owned and nodded with approval. If you wanted a business to succeed in a village then you often had to diversify, and Ellie had definitely serviced the demand in a variety of areas. The wafting scent of newly baked bread, arranged in rows behind the counter, greeted customers. The patisserie selection of fancy cakes behind the glass front of the counter was brightly colourful, and the shelves all around the café were brimming with jams and marmalades for customers to purchase. Each label had a white background and a picture of a blue Cornish pixie with his hand in a jam jar, and Ellie's store brand clearly displayed her logo which read, *Pixie's Place, Bakery & Tea Room.*

"So, how are things going apart from the jam? How're Gregory and the children doing?"

Morgana was very fond of her nephew and nieces, and her brother-in-law too, even though he was quite sceptical when it came to anything paranormal. Unfortunately for him, anything paranormal locally encompassed his wife and her siblings.

A flicker of a frown passed across Ellie's face.

"What is it?" Morgana asked. "Are the children okay?"

"Oh yes, of course, everybody's fine."

"Then what was that look for? Come on, Ellie, you can tell me. Is it Gregory? Witching and gossiping is what sisters do."

Ellie gave a small, dismissive shrug. "It's nothing really. We've just had a few rows recently. Business stuff mostly. I wanted to pay Harry a little more since his work is incredibly good, but…"

Morgana nodded sympathetically. It was tough for Ellie because although her business made a profit, it didn't make a lot, and the person behind the business with the money was Gregory. He owned a chain of bakeries back in his hometown of Bristol, where it was much easier to turn a profit with continuous trade; unlike their seaside village in Cornwall where the trade could be very seasonal.

"Are you not paying Harry what he's worth? Or is it something else?" Morgana's eyes twinkled as she made to tease her sister. "I mean he is rather a hottie, not to mention extremely talented in the kitchen. Is Gregory feeling threatened by a younger man spending so much time with you?"

Ellie gave a brief laugh at that idea. "Of course not! Don't be silly. Greg and I certainly have no problems in that direction."

Morgana nodded. She knew that Gregory and Ellie were devoted to each other, and it was such a surprise to hear that they'd had any kind of tiff. They never rowed at all, normally.

"Is there anyone else skirting around Harry? Or anyone he seems to like?" Morgana asked as innocently as she was able.

Ellie laughed again. "Apart from you? No, not as far as I've seen, though he's only been here a month. I think that market is wide open if you were thinking of finally taking an interest in men again? I wouldn't wait too long if I were you. Mum says that Morwenna might be coming home sometime soon, and we both know she'd be all over that one. And he's made it clear he likes you so he might also like her?"

It was Morgana's turn to frown. Whilst she loved her twin sister, she could only take Morwenna in very small doses and the news of any upcoming visit didn't exactly fill her with joy. They might be identical twins in looks, but their personalities were total opposites.

"Ugh, you're right there. I think your new pâtissier would definitely catch her attention with those brooding good looks and those sexy dark eyes." Morgana's gaze slid over to the counter where Harry had just made an appearance with a tray of éclairs which he was now laying out artfully behind the display glass.

Morgana sniffed the air and let out a small moan of appreciation. "He really is an absolute whiz with those fancy-pants cakes. I simply cannot imagine why he's burying his talent here in Portmage."

"Because this is the most beautiful place in the world?" Ellie suggested, totally biased. "It happens every year, doesn't it? People come here on holiday from the city and get a breath of our sea air, rugged coastline, and sandy beaches, and they fall in love with the place and never leave it again."

Morgana nodded because it was quite true. There were many people in the village who had left the city behind for the simpler life by the sea.

"Like your Gregory for example," Morgana agreed. "But still, I'm guessing you're not paying Harry anything close to London wages?"

"No, you're quite right, we're not," Ellie made a face. "But as Greg pointed out, life here isn't anywhere near as expensive as London. Harry gets to live in a charming cottage overlooking Pixie Cove and it still only costs about a quarter of the price of renting a one bed flat in London. So it's all relative, isn't it?"

"Absolutely. Even just compared to the years I spent living in Bath, Portmage is far cheaper and has so much to offer if you like that kind of life." Morgana gave an appreciative look through the window at the windswept High Street outside, and felt a wave of satisfaction at being able to live and work in a place she loved so dearly. She shifted her attention back to the counter as she heard a giggle of laughter and saw Harry being charming to Mrs. Cantrell. It was quite a shock to see Mrs. Cantrell smile. The woman was a battleaxe of nearly 90 years of age and Morgana generally found her quite ferocious. She'd often witnessed the old woman shouting at tourists for parking their cars in front of her house, terrifying them into quickly moving onward.

"You know what? I think I'm going to take your advice and make an effort to say hello and strike while the iron's hot, or at least before the wicked witch gets back into town," she said, referring to her other sister. "And I have a sudden hankering for a chocolate éclair." Morgana gave Ellie a conspiratorial wink and rose to her feet.

Morgana approached the counter slowly, surreptitiously smoothing down her long dark hair. It had been a little while since she last had a love interest. Mainly because pickings were a little slim on the ground in the village where they lived. There had been a few dates with Jamie Fenchurch just before Christmas, but she hadn't really felt ready for a new relationship and it had never taken off. She blamed her ex-boyfriend Ryan for that. Her last serious relationship had left her feeling pretty bruised when it hadn't ended well. Which was a total understatement.

Of course that was when she'd acquired the true love of her life, her cat Lancelot. It was certainly a trade she would make any day so it hadn't been all bad.

Harry looked up and gave Morgana a warm smile as she drew nearer and her pulse jumped a little as he ran his long fingers through his shiny black hair, pushing it back off his face. She watched captivated as the hair instantly sprang back into place, curling adorably over his forehead.

"Good Morning, Morgana. Can I tempt you with

anything today?" He gestured towards the gorgeous looking pastries he had just arranged.

"Yes, you certainly can, these all look delicious. Are both types of éclair chocolate?"

"These are chocolate," he pointed to the ones with a dark brown top, "and those are coffee and caramel." He pointed out the other type which had a lighter top.

"Coffee and caramel? Sounds wonderful. One of them to take away please, and what are these tarts?"

"Tarte Tatin, that's apple. Tarte Abricot which is apricot, and the Tarte aux Poires." He leaned forward and said in a sotto voice, "The pears are soaked overnight in Cointreau, which is what really enhances the flavour. Then I burn off the alcohol and it caramelises the pears at the same time."

"One of those as well then," she said, already feeling her mouth-watering, "to take away, please."

"Let me know if you like it as it's one of my favourites." An oven dinged behind him and he gave an apologetic smile before handing over her package and hurrying back into the kitchen.

Morgana went back to Ellie. "He looks as yummy as his food does."

"I'm glad you think so. If you got together, then it's another reason for him to stay in the area. Just don't mess it up," Ellie ribbed her.

"Humph, I can't guarantee that. Did you see how red the sky was this morning?"

"*Red sky at night, shepherds delight. Red sky in the morning, shepherds warning*," Ellie quoted the old proverb. "It just means we have some bad weather coming."

"It might be more than that since it's the 1st of May

today."

"Oh yes, of course. Happy Beltane. I should get some yellow flowers. It's a good time for a fresh start and maybe a fresh relationship?" Ellie gave Morgana a nudge.

"Yeah, maybe. Or it could be a warning about the fact that Morwenna is coming and we should all flee the village."

Ellie tutted at her. "You say it like her return is on par with a demon apocalypse."

"That just about sums it up," Morgana agreed.

Chapter Two

Taking her second breakfast neatly boxed up, Morgana found her feet walking her back towards the sea. Back to the high cliff of the headland that jutted out at the far end of Portmage village. It was still early, and the path had yet to fill up with the usual walkers and tourists who'd appear later in the day. For now, she was able to enjoy the majesty of the scene before her undisturbed. A dark blue sea with white-tipped waves stretched out as far as the eye could see. A few colourful buoys bobbed in the water and there were a couple of sailboats just visible on the horizon.

It was a view to die for but as Morgana stood there feeling the wind in her hair, her brow furrowed. She thought about the colour of the sea that morning. It wouldn't normally bother her, but it was the 1st of May. And for those with a witchy inclination, the May Day dawn was significant. It was the start of summer, a time of change, and Morgana gave a small shudder as her eyes fell on Portmage Castle and the long shadow it cast. The shadow seemed to be reaching for her and she took an inadvertent step backward.

The castle was just a ruin on a jutting-out peninsular accessed only by a narrow strip of cliff that connected it to the mainland, but it still looked foreboding and impressive. Only one of its original four towers still stood, but the outer walls of the castle were intact. A testament to the men who constructed it some thousand plus years earlier. Now it was just a tourist attraction. The alleged birthplace of the great King Arthur, and of her namesake and ancestor too. Which was probably why she felt so connected to it, no matter how unwillingly.

Morgana averted her eyes from the castle and busied herself by cutting a few long switches of hawthorn from a bush that grew wild beside the path. It was filled with bright and cheerful yellow flowers, and she thought they'd make a nice decoration for her shop.

"Good morning, Miss Emrys," a cultured voice rang out with just a hint of condemnation in the tone. It made her feel as if she'd just been caught doing something naughty by a Headmistress.

"Mrs. Goodbody." She inclined her head to the woman striding along the path with a West Highland Terrier at her heels. The little dog was attempting to sniff every rabbit hole on the way, but his mistress was relentlessly pulling him onwards on a short lead. He gave a yip of joy as Mrs. Goodbody stopped to speak to Morgana. It gave him the chance to pee on a pretty cluster of daffodils.

"Lovely morning for a stroll, brisk but bright," Mrs. Goodbody declared, using her usual opening gambit of commenting on the weather. "But you must be chilly, dear. Did you forget to bring a coat?" She looked Morgana up and down seemingly content with the length of her dress but her lips tightened as she looked pointedly at Morgana's low neckline.

Morgana resisted the urge to make a pithy reply. She knew that Mrs. Goodbody took a delight in disapproving of her clothes in general, and didn't want to give her the satisfaction of becoming offended. Morgana liked to embrace her witchy heritage in her dresses, and today's number was a grey velvet with scoop neck and a swirly pleated hem and batwing sleeves.

"You're quite right, Mrs. Goodbody, a coat would have been a good idea. And perhaps my witch's hat."

Oh well, she'd tried not to, but sometimes she couldn't help herself.

Mrs. Goodbody sucked in a large breath and straightened her back. "Just remember, Morgana, a gentle woman is a woman to love. You don't want to scare every man away, do you?"

"No, Mrs. Goodbody," Morgana said as meekly as she was able, while valiantly suppressing her laughter.

"Perhaps a nice cardigan would be the answer. You could keep it on even when you're indoors too." Mrs. Goodbody gave another disapproving sniff at Morgana's exposed neckline and tugged on her dogs' leash. "Come Horace, no dawdling."

Morgana gathered the switches of hawthorn in her arms and followed at a more leisurely pace.

"*A gentle woman is a woman to love,*" she muttered to herself in amusement. "Her husband was absolutely terrified of her. Poor man spent every spare moment in his greenhouse hiding. Gentle? Humph." She picked up her pace when Mrs. Goodbody took a right toward the castle, the opposite direction that Morgana was heading.

Behind her the path eventually wound down to Pixie Cove, a beach covered in pebbles, and renowned for its seals and its surf. The path going left went back to Portmage, the Cornish village where she lived. Walking back to the village, she glanced down the opposite side of the cliff where the long sandy stretch of Portmage beach was already beginning to attract dog walkers. A couple of fishing boats could be seen coming in with the catch of the day.

Fishing had once been the main industry in Lower Portmage, but it was a tough business and few sustained it these days. Upper Portmage was the hub of the village now. The long High Street was brimming with shops of various kinds, most trading on the tourists who came for the castle. Just as she did herself. She'd been lucky enough to secure shop premises on the most coveted bit of real estate between the main car park and the path to the castle, which meant that the majority of tourists had to walk right past her door if they wanted to visit the ancient ruin. On the far side of the parking area, the road curved one way to continue the High Street and the other way went down the hill to Lower Portmage.

Morgana walked past the local pub, The Knights at Arms, and a jewellers before stopping briefly at the newsagents to pick up the daily paper. She paused next in front of a clothes shop, The Squire's Domain, and admired a long red peasant skirt. Positioning her body so it was placed right in front of her own reflection, she tried to work out if it would suit her.

At 5ft 8", she was taller than a lot of women, including Ellie, but unlike her older sister Morgana was still quite slim. She saw that her long brown tresses were looking decidedly windswept after her early jaunt along the cliff path, and she raised a hand to smooth her hair back down again.

"Great look, scarecrow chic." She admonished her reflection. But on the whole the image pleased her. Her long black boots went rather well with the red skirt, but she preferred the dress she was already wearing. She leaned forward to check the price sticker through the glass and then shook her head decisively.

"That much money would keep Lancelot in fresh tuna for a year."

She continued on past The Round Table, which was a rather nice seafood restaurant. Then past the sweet shop, an antiques shop, and a beauty salon until she reached her own place of business, Merlin's Attic.

Merlin's Attic was a small shop on a corner with whitewashed outer walls and mullioned windows. Like so many other businesses in Portmage, it capitalised on the Arthurian theme of the village and sold all kinds of witchy goods. In the window, there was a large fairy-tale castle made of wood, a bowl full of semi-precious gemstones, some Celtic silver rings, and a few books on magic and local legends. But the sight that pleased her most was seeing her black cat sitting right by the glass looking almost like a stuffed animal, except for the slight twitching of his whiskers as he watched the passers-by. As soon as he spotted Morgana, he left his sentry post and jumped down to greet her at the door.

"Lancelot, you almost seem pleased to see me," she teased, bending to rub behind his ear. "It's very un-catlike behaviour."

He gave her a supercilious look and then sniffed at the box in her hands.

"Ah, I get it now. You're wondering if I've brought you anything to eat. You've already had breakfast, you greedy feline." But she moved to the shop counter and opened the drawer fishing out a handful of cat treats anyway.

"Right, we open in ten minutes so let's get things moving," she said, switching on her cash register and a few alcove lights. Merlin's Attic had a deliberately eclectic layout so that shoppers could browse and then stumble upon unexpected corners. The point was to make them feel that they'd discovered treasures that others had missed. There was even an old steamer trunk that was kept shut. But if anyone happened to open it, they found it full of goblets and plates that were made of Cornish tin and all marked down on sale. They were some of her biggest sellers and she had to restock the trunk almost every night during the height of the season.

The final step before opening the door for business was to cleanse the space of any residual energy from the day before. She walked anti-clockwise around the shop carrying a smoking sage stick. Then she swept the entire floor with her old-fashioned broom brushing the collected dust out the front door onto the street where it quickly blew away in the constant sea wind.

"Dust to dust," Morgana intoned playfully and then felt a weird chill go down the back of her neck. "Okay, that red dawn has me a bit spooked," she explained to the cat.

Lancelot licked his nose in response and stared at her.

"Yes, you're right, mama is bat-crap crazy." She kissed the top of his head and opened the daily newspaper on the countertop beside him. Morgana scanned the news as a matter of course, but didn't take much of it in. The real reason she bought the paper was to do the crossword.

"A dastardly stratagem, four letters," she read aloud.

"A plan? No, a plot." She'd barely filled in the first word when some customers came into the shop. This was the real point of the crossword. Nobody liked to be stared at by a shopkeeper while they browsed so it gave her a way to be available but disinterested. She already knew from long experience that the British tourist quickly left if you approached them, whereas the American wanted you on-hand at all times. She kept her ears alert and picked up a German accent, so she looked up and smiled brightly. Germans didn't waste hours browsing and not buying. They were good spenders, but they also didn't want any help. She returned to the crossword as soon as she'd made eye contact letting them know she'd be available when they were ready. She just hoped it wouldn't be too soon because as much as the crossword was a prop, she was also a bit of an addict. She thought of it as her 'personal war'. A battle to be won by completing it, and customers were an unwelcome interruption at times.

After the Germans, she had two teenage girls who left their parents outside and came in full of enthusiasm for the quirkiness of her stock.

"My kind of customers," she told Lancelot out of the side of her mouth.

The girls blew almost their entire holiday budget on some wind-chimes for their parent's anniversary gift, and several bronze pixies as presents for their friends back home, so Morgana chucked in two sun-catchers free of charge for their bedrooms. The sun-catchers were popular because when you hung them in a window, they filled the entire room with rainbows as the sun passed through the crystal. The girls were thrilled, and one of them immediately began posting pictures and a glowing review on her social media accounts.

"Told you so!" Morgana said smugly to Lancelot as the girls left.

And so the day went by. There were lulls but not many as it was the May Bank Holiday weekend after all, and Morgana worked right through until five pm without a break.

"I'm thinking we should probably hire some help when the summer holiday comes around," Morgana commented to the cat. She thought about how Ellie had two waitresses to help her, plus Harry in the kitchen, not to mention the fact that Gregory did all the accounts for her. The trouble was that Merlin's Attic was so very much her own place that she'd struggle with letting anyone else have input.

Lancelot thought of nothing but his stomach, and sat pointedly on the steps that led up to the flat they lived in above the shop.

"I know, I know, it's closing time." She rose to lock the door, but was only halfway there when a large family came in. Their accent was instantly recognisable as being from Birmingham, and there were far more children than parents. Morgana grimaced as the children instantly made for some shiny silver goblets which would no doubt soon be covered in sticky fingerprints.

"Kitty!" the smallest girl exclaimed rushing toward Lancelot, who did nothing to live up to his heroic name and promptly bolted under the serving counter.

"Deserter," Morgana whispered, poking him with her foot.

"Don't you have any postcards?" the father asked, looking around with a frown.

"No, sorry." She kept a fixed smile on her face. "The newsagents might still be open if you're quick."

Please, please leave and go to the newsagents, she thought, feeling guilty for wishing it on them instead.

"We're not here to buy overpriced knick-knacks," he informed his wife crossly as she began to sniff various packets of incense.

There was a noise of something dropping heavily to the floor, and Morgana whirled to check on the children.

"Kevin, put that down," the father bellowed then strode over to grab a child who resisted. The two of them engaged in a tug of war with Kevin's arm in the middle, until the father won. He picked up the child who then kicked out and knocked down a bowl filled with tiny wooden animals.

Morgana's hand went automatically to the crystal around her neck. She mumbled a quick protective incantation wishing she'd spent more time on her wards that morning. *It served her right for being complacent,* she thought. Tomorrow she'd double her preparation, but in the meantime how long would she have to keep calm?

Her nerves were almost at breaking point as she watched Kevin kick a few more times, when the mother suddenly decided to intervene. "Come along, all of you out."

The tone of authority took instant effect and the children all turned and followed her from the shop. Morgana waited to see if the father would apologise as he herded them from the rear, but he didn't even meet her eye.

She exhaled deeply before going down to her hands and knees to start picking up the wooden animals.

"And they didn't even buy anything. Remind me not to have *five* kids anytime soon," she grumbled, confident in the notion that Ellie would never allow her three children to run amok like that while she blissfully browsed.

She muttered a few choice words under her breath as the bell on the door chimed again and she realised she still hadn't locked it. She turned slowly, looking up from her position on the floor, and caught Harry admiring her backside. He instantly averted his gaze to the ceiling instead.

"Harry," she said, trying to smother her laugh. "What can I do for you?"

He ran his hand through his hair, almost nervously this time. "Ellie thought… that is, I was wondering about dinner sometime? Or perhaps, just a drink to start if you want to, but you might not…" he trailed off, looking charmingly unsure.

"Yes."

"Yes?"

"Yes, I'd love to have a drink with you. I was thinking of going out for one tonight as it happens, just down to the pub. It's usually good fun in there on a Saturday evening, though it will probably be packed." She didn't say that she would feel far more comfortable in a busy lively pub than sitting quietly in a restaurant together. She didn't know if they had anything in common yet, apart from the fact he was gorgeous. She thought he must like her too seeing as how he was asking her out, even if her sister had annoyingly interfered to make it happen.

"Tonight, great." He relaxed slightly. "I need to go

home and shower after sweating over a hot oven all day first though."

"You smell fantastic, if that counts for anything. Like warm donuts. But yes, I want to wash the day out of my hair too, and we should probably eat before we meet as we'll never get a table for food. So, would eightish suit you?"

He agreed with this and went on his way while Morgana turned excitedly to Lancelot. "I have a date! It's been ages since my last one. What if I've forgotten how? Didn't you think he was cute?" She tickled the cat under the chin.

Lancelot looked disdainful and gave a hungry meow in response.

"Right, of course," she laughed. "Dinner first, I get it."

They went upstairs and Morgana set about feeding Lancelot and making herself a wrap, followed by the pear tart. Then a long cleansing bath, where she soaked in the bubbles until her tired feet stopped aching.

By eight o'clock, she was pushing her way through the crowd in the pub and her spirits were lifted high by the hubbub of cheerful voices and the bright smile of Harry waiting at the bar.

"What can I get you?" he asked, indicating the barman already handing him a drink.

"Dry white wine, please."

"Muscadet, if you have it," Harry told the barman.

Morgana gave him an approving nod. "You know your wine?"

"French wine, I do. It's just a shame that I don't really drink." He held up his own glass and she saw that it contained a pint of cola.

"Oh!" She looked guiltily at the large glass being poured for her. "Then how do you know?"

"I trained in Paris. France is the only place to go if you want to work as a Pâtissier. They take their pastries very seriously."

"And then you returned to England? Nobody special to keep you there?"

He gave her a knowing grin. "Is that a subtle way of asking about my love life? One ex-wife, nobody since then."

"Oh dear, sorry to hear that."

"It's not a big deal. We were both too young to think through what we were doing." He shrugged it off. "So, how about you? Any burly boyfriends who I should watch my back around?" He paid for their drinks and then turned around scanning the room for a table but pretending to check out the competition.

Morgana laughed, "Not for a while now. Most of the guys here think I'm weird."

"I like weird."

"And I like a man who can cook," Morgana returned the compliment. "Didn't your wife appreciate that?" She fished for a little more information.

"I think she'd have preferred a man with more money," he said dryly, gesturing to a table by the window where a couple were just getting to their feet. Once they'd sat down, he changed the subject. "This is pretty, do the charms mean anything?" He tapped the charm bracelet she wore on her wrist.

"Actually, they do." Morgana turned the bracelet fondly in the lamp light. "I'm sure you're already familiar with the Celtic triple knot, and this one is the tree of life. Then the Maiden, Mother and Crone." She touched each as she named it. "The cat is supposed to be my own, Lancelot; this swirly one is the symbol of Merlin; and lastly a Cornish Pixie, of course."

"Ah yes, like Ellie's bakery. I've often wondered why it's called Pixie's Place and not Ellie's Place? Is it named after Pixie Cove?"

"Pixie is actually her middle name, though I strongly suspect she was conceived at Pixie Cove."

"It is pretty romantic down there, especially at this time of year when the sea is so fierce. You should come and visit me sometime in the cottage I'm renting. My front windows look right out over the beach." He gave her a long look and Morgana felt warm under his gaze.

"Yes, maybe," she hedged, not wanting to rush into anything.

"I can cook more than cakes; I make a wonderful Coq au Vin with pearl shallots and baby button mushrooms. The seafood around here is also fantastic. Last week I bought some spider crabs right off the boats as they came in and ate them dripping with garlic butter."

Morgana felt hungry just hearing him describe food, especially as he made it sound so sensual. It was only going to take him mere hours to crack through her defences at this rate.

"Do you get much time to surf too? I think Ellie said you moved here for the waves?" She asked, trying to shake off the temptation to suggest they return to his cottage immediately.

"Yes, Pixie Cove is perfect for that too. I have to start pretty early each morning at the bakery, but it means I'm usually finished by two or three so I get plenty of time to get in the water. You'll have to tell me about other good beaches around here. I haven't had much time yet to get familiar with the area."

The next couple of hours passed easily as they chatted about local places to visit until Morgana decided to call it a night as she was exhausted after her early start and a busy Saturday in the shop.

Harry insisted on walking her back to Merlin's Attic, but he didn't suggest coming in. Instead he merely commented that he hoped they'd do it again soon, before heading back in the opposite direction.

"Quite a successful evening," Morgana informed Lancelot as she changed into her nightwear. "He's sexy but not pushy which is an ideal combination for me right now. After that debacle with Ryan…" she gave a shudder, remembering her last serious boyfriend. "Maybe this summer will be pretty good after all."

She fell into a deep and happy sleep until she was rudely awakened by the insistent ringing of her phone. Rubbing her eyes, she looked blearily at her bedside clock.

5.30 am?

"Somebody had better be dead," she barked crossly into the phone as she picked it up.

"They are," came Ellie's quavering voice. "There's a body in my bakery."

Chapter Three

Morgana didn't get much more out of Ellie. Only that she'd already called the police, but she was terrified and Greg was away for work.

"Sit tight, I'm on my way," Morgana reassured her sister. Less than five minutes later, she was hurrying down the road towards the bakery. Peering through the window, she saw Ellie sitting at one of the cafe tables inside looking white and rigid with shock.

Ellie stood up and let Morgana in noting the way Morgana's eyes swept the room.

"She's in the kitchen." Ellie's voice was flat and emotionless.

Ellie went to push open the swing door that led to the kitchen, but Morgana put a hand on her arm stopping her. "I don't think we're supposed to touch anything since the police will want to take fingerprints."

"Bit late for that. I had to open this door before I found her." Ellie pushed the door and then stood back so Morgana could see inside. Morgana stepped carefully past Ellie and then stopped short. She didn't need to go any further. The body of a young woman was on the floor. Her feet were still in the walk-in fridge and her arms sprawled awkwardly out into the prep area.

"She was in the fridge. When I opened it, she just fell out," Ellie continued to speak in a tone that was totally devoid of emotion.

"Oh, Ells, what a scare. Do you have any idea who

she is?"

Ellie shook her head helplessly.

"Okay, do you know how she got in there? I suppose she must have frozen to death?"

Ellie shook her head again, her hand going to her throat. Morgana caught on immediately and took another tentative step into the room. She could see the woman more clearly now. Vibrant blonde hair, attractive features, and an ugly red bruise in a line around her neck. Clearly the woman had been strangled with something.

Morgana resisted the urge to move the woman into a more comfortable position, because despite being dead, her body was lying unnaturally and it just seemed so wrong. Before she could act on the instinct, there came a hammering on the bakery door.

"Sit down. I'll deal with it," Morgana instructed Ellie, who dutifully did as she was bade. A sure sign that she wasn't in her right mind.

"Good morning. We had a 999 call from here indicating that someone had been murdered?" The man looked like he didn't believe the words for a moment.

"That's right." Morgana narrowed her eyes at him suspiciously, having expected someone in uniform.

He correctly interpreted her look and reached into his coat, bringing out a badge. "DS Treharne."

"Come in." She held the door wide and he stepped inside, whereupon Morgana did a double take. "Tristan?"

Tristan Treharne, previously known to her as the bad boy of the local secondary school, wearing a suit? Two years older than Morgana, he'd been the one they all sighed over in his leather jacket and daredevil ripped jeans. He'd been a heartbreaker back then, only getting his comeuppance during his torrid on-again-off-again relationship with Morgana's twin sister, Morwenna. Morwenna had kicked his heart around like a football until she had ended it once and for all and he'd left town in a puff of motorbike smoke. And now he was back as an officer of the law? Morgana felt her own heart kick before firmly squashing it.

His eyes swept the room taking in Ellie and then Morgana.

"Elaine Emrys, and…" he paused, clearly trying to decide which sister she was. "Morgana?" He looked hesitant, waiting for her answer.

She favoured him with a warm smile for getting it right and nodded. "Ellie is Elaine Westbrook now. She's married." Her eyes travelled down to his ring finger, but it was bare. Not that that meant anything.

"And she's the one who made the call? A *murder*?" he still sounded disbelieving.

"In here," she pushed again at the kitchen door allowing him to go in ahead of her. He took a second to kneel beside the girl on the floor, his face now grim and serious.

Morgana took the chance to appraise him while he wasn't looking. After all, it had been ten years. He was still ridiculously handsome with hair and eyes the colour of melted chocolate, broad facial features that were too big but that all worked together. There also an intriguing scar over one eyebrow and he looked even better than before now that he was all grown up. She was sad about the absence of his trademark leather jacket though. She wondered how on earth the bad boy, who showed every sign of ending up in prison one day, had ended up in law enforcement instead.

"I'm going to call my DI, and I want you both to stay in the front okay?" Tristan pushed Morgana out of the kitchen and firmly shut the door. She could hear him talking in animated tones to various people while she and Ellie waited. Eventually he came back out.

"He's on his way, but I'd like to ask a few preliminary questions if you don't mind?" He pulled a chair up to their table.

"Of course." Morgana gave him a searching look. "So, you're a sergeant now?"

"Detective Sergeant. You probably ought to address me as DS Treharne while I'm working. I'm with the Criminal Investigation Department." Tristan puffed out his chest a little and Morgana stifled the urge to poke fun at him for his radical change of character.

"Okay, but you still check out all the random calls that come in?" She couldn't resist pushing his buttons just a smidge.

He exhaled, letting the bravado go out of his stance. "I was in the area staying with my mother for the night. There's only a couple of Constables at Westpoint Police Station, so I thought I'd help out by answering this call. I didn't actually think I'd find a murder though. I've called my Detective Inspector to come over from Bodmin."

"Oh, well I'm sorry we disturbed your morning."

He leaned forward looking less official and more like the boy she used to know as he gave her a brief flash of a smile. "This is what I've been trained to deal with, so it's probably just as well you've got me. It means we can get started straight away. Let's begin with who the deceased is?"

Morgana looked at Ellie checking to see if her sister was talking yet. So far she'd been very quiet, which wasn't like her at all. Ellie sensed the look and shook herself out of her funk.

"I don't know. I've no idea who she is, I've never seen her before. I came in to open up and there she was inside the walk-in. I suppose someone must have broken in during the night, but I can't think who…" she trailed off as though an idea had just struck her.

"What? Did you remember something?" Tristan asked, obviously perceiving her change of expression.

Ellie blinked, then stared at Tristan, registering him properly for the first time. "You're Tristan Treharne. Didn't you used to go out with Morwenna?"

"A very long time ago. Now, about what you just thought of?"

"And Bradley Treharne is your younger brother?" Ellie ignored his question in favour of one of her own.

Tristan sighed, "Yes, and I expect my mother comes into the bakery on occasion too. Could we get back to the girl in your fridge? You were saying there must have been a break-in?"

"I didn't think to check." Ellie's face had gone vacant again. "I came in through the front, started getting out what we needed, and remembered that the bread wouldn't be made fresh because it was Sunday. So I went to get it from the fridge and when I opened the door, she fell out."

"Shall I go and examine the back door? See if it's been forced or anything?" Morgana offered, getting to her feet.

"Absolutely not, the kitchen is a crime scene now,

you can't go back in there." Tristan gave her a firm shake of the head and Morgana subsided back into her chair.

"Hang on," Ellie became alert again. "You can't keep us out of the kitchen. I need to retrieve the food for the customers."

"I'm sorry, Mrs. Westbrook, but you won't be able to open today, and not for a while I should think. In fact, until we've established how she actually got into the fridge, the entire premises will be cordoned off. I expect the Inspector will want to question you at the station, or perhaps at your home, but you won't be able to open the bakery until the forensics team have completely finished with it. That can be several days or even weeks if necessary."

"You don't sound very sure," Morgana snapped, hating the sight of the fear and bewilderment that now filled Ellie's eyes.

Tristan gave an apologetic gesture with his hands. "This is the first murder we've had since I returned. Most of the crime around here is drunk drivers and petty theft. Stay put, I'll go and check the back door."

"Can I make Ellie a cup of tea? And one for you too?" she offered hopefully.

But Tristan shook his head. "It's better if you don't touch anything."

When he'd gone, Morgana put her hand over Ellie's. "You said Gregory is away? Can I call him for you?"

"He's in Bristol, visiting his other businesses. I rang his hotel early this morning but there was no answer from his room."

"That's odd. Never mind, I'm sure he'll call you soon enough. Where are the children?"

"They stayed over with mum last night because I had such an early start. Normally I would leave them with Greg, but with him away...Sunday is Harry's day off, and he's usually the one who opens up. He would have found the body instead of me. Why did it have to happen today of all days?"

"I don't know sweetie, I'm sorry. You'll probably have to answer some more questions, but then I'll take you down to mum's house, okay? It will be a day off for you. Maybe you can even have a family Sunday lunch with the kids?"

Ellie gave a weak smile. "I bet I end up being the one making the Sunday lunch. You know how mum is, she probably gave them ice-cream for breakfast."

Morgana chuckled at the memory of similar childhood breakfasts. Their mother was lovely, but also rather disorganised and vague about remembering mealtimes. She was always absorbed in her artwork and forgot to open her little gallery half the time, especially if she was in the middle of painting. Her home was a fun place with very few rules. Except one, no touching the art!

"They'll be enjoying it immensely," Morgana assured her sister.

Tristan came back looking almost relieved. "Yes, you've definitely had a break-in. The catch on the window is damaged. I think someone climbed in and then opened the back door from the inside. It's a lot of trouble to go to if you didn't know the place, and a strange location to hide a body. Can you think of anyone at all who might have a grudge against you?"

Ellie opened her mouth to speak and then shut it

again.

Morgana gave her a side glance but only said, "Hopefully whoever it was will have left some fingerprints or some other incriminating evidence. It's not easy to climb through a window without touching anything."

At that moment a car pulled up outside and Morgana recognised Detective Inspector Aiden Lowen getting out of it. She'd met him once before, six months earlier when there had been another murder in the village. She wondered now where Tristan had been at the time.

Morgana eyed the Inspector warily as he spoke again briefly with Tristan and then came over to her and Ellie.

"Miss Emrys." Detective Inspector Lowen gave her an unreadable look.

"How nice to see you again," she said, her voice filled with insincerity.

She thought she saw a flicker of a smile in his eyes, but he just inclined his head in acknowledgment of her words.

He was a formidable man in his late fifties, with an ex-military stance, a hard jaw and hints of grey at his temples. His eyes were as dark as his skin, and he had a way about him that suggested he saw everything despite his outward calm demeanour.

Morgana got the impression he suspected Ellie of some involvement in the murder despite the very gentle tone he used to extract a great deal of information through open questions.

Not long after him came a third police officer, this time a Constable in uniform. PC Poppy Dunn had been in the same class as Morgana at school and she crashed through the door looking harried and distinctly unkempt. Morgana hid a smile as she decided that Poppy had been rudely awoken to be there, just as she herself had. Poppy immediately set about securing the scene and tried to hide her yawns. Morgana was sure that Poppy needed a lot more coffee to make the early start acceptable, and she had her full sympathy on that count.

Only after the Inspector had taken contact details for everyone who worked there did he eventually let Morgana take Ellie away. They stopped first at Morgana's where she fed the cat and tried to insist that Ellie eat too. Ellie refused anything but a cup of tea and tried to ring Gregory again. His mobile phone went straight to voicemail, but his hotel was able to confirm that he had checked out some half an hour earlier.

"Well, that's something," Morgana said bracingly as Ellie continued to look worried. "He's probably on his way home, and if he isn't, then he soon will be when he gets your message. So until then, we'll go and get the children and enjoy the day okay?"

"But what about the bakery?" Ellie protested.

"Ells, there is nothing you can do about that. You'll get word when you can go back in, but in the meantime, you have to think of it as an enforced holiday."

"What about your shop? You can't close just because I am."

"I can do what I want," Morgana said forcefully. "And I want to spend the day with my sister. I'll put a note on the door and that's that."

Ellie meekly nodded and nibbled at the edge of a piece of toast. There was silence for a while as Morgana got stuck into breakfast, but then Ellie asked in a quiet voice, "Who do you think she is?"

"The body? No idea. She's not local I'm sure of it. Plus, did you notice that her hair had been recently done? None of the nearby salons could have managed such a posh hairdo, and her nails were pretty perfect too so I'd say she'd just had a manicure as well. City girl, I think."

"She looked so young and pretty too."

"Make-up can do wonders, but I think she was closer to thirty, about your age," Morgana said, cuttingly.

"Be nice, Mog, she's dead."

Morgana shrugged, "It's not as though we knew her." For some reason, she felt inexplicably cross with the dead girl for showing up in Ellie's business. Then changed her mind as she realised she was far more cross with whoever had put her there.

"I hope they catch the person who murdered her quickly," Ellie gave a shudder, clearly thinking along the same lines as Morgana.

"Me too. Murder is not the nicest way to start the day. Have some more tea."

Ellie looked thoughtful as she pushed her cup forward. "It was weird seeing Tristan Treharne acting all official. Do you remember what a trouble-maker he used to be?"

"Do I ever," Morgana grinned. "He once stole Old Marley's tractor and drove it all over the moors. It had to be winched out of a bog in the end. He was extremely lucky Marley made him work off the costs instead of having him arrested." She didn't add that she and a gaggle of girlfriends used to sneak onto the farm to watch Tristan stacking the hay bales with his shirt off. Of course, it wasn't long after that Morwenna started going out with him which firmly put paid to any romantic feelings Morgana might have had.

"He left here when he turned eighteen didn't he? I thought he'd gone off to seek his fortune. Either that or become a drug addict, and now he's back as a *Detective* no less?"

"Stranger things have happened, though not many," Morgana agreed. "Of course, someone stuffing a girl in your walk-in is pretty strange. It's almost malicious to have chosen the bakery when there must have been a whole host of easier places. Are you sure you have no idea who it could be?"

For the second time that day, Ellie opened her mouth and then closed it again before dropping her head into her hands. "I don't know. I just wish Greg was here."

Ellie's voice was tearful and Morgana decided not to push her. She'd been through enough for one morning. But she was also convinced that Ellie was holding something back. She pondered that as they walked down to their mother's house. Why would Ellie keep her mouth shut if she had any suspicions about the murder? Or more importantly, why would Ellie withhold information? Who was she trying to protect?

Chapter Four

Ellie and Morgana opted to drive down to Lower Portmage despite the fact it was an easy walk from the main village at the top of the cliff down the road to the bay, or via the steep steps down the cliff and then across the beach. The issue was that they may be bringing the children back with them and Ellie's youngest, Martha, was not yet old enough to manage the walk back up to Portmage, at least not without an awful lot of whining on the way.

Ellie, who had never really left Portmage, hadn't ever bothered to buy a car of her own so they took Morgana's Land Rover. Morgana loved her Land Rover as though it were family. Despite the racket it made, and the fact that it bounced and bumped along the roads, it had a lot of boot space and was ideal for packing plenty of stock into the back. Also, Morgana never had to worry about it getting endlessly splashed with mud on the country roads around the village. It was a noisy beast that could handle anything, anything except long journeys, as it guzzled petrol at an alarming rate.

Five minutes later, Morgana pulled the car up at the back entrance of the art gallery that her mother owned and lived in. Lower Portmage was a pretty little bay with high cliffs on both sides and a long sweep of sandy beach dividing them. While the main hub of the village was at the top of the hill, the lower part was still popular with tourists and provided another pub, a cafe, a fishmonger, a surf shop, and their mother's art gallery.

They were greeted by the smiling face of their mother Delia, a woman of nearly sixty with her hair already silver, but she was still strikingly beautiful and her face was practically unlined though covered in freckles from the sun.

"Hello, my darlings," she spread her arms wide to encompass her two daughters and hugged them both soundly. "Was I expecting you this early?"

"No mother," Ellie shook her head. "There's been an incident at the bakery and I wasn't able to open today. Morgana very kindly said she would keep me company until it's been sorted."

"Oh well, the children will be delighted I'm sure." Delia ushered them both inside where they found the three children, Daniel, Chloe and Martha, seated around the breakfast table enjoying a brunch of pancakes and maple syrup.

"At least it's not ice cream," Morgana whispered to Ellie. Ellie gave her a weak smile in return and hugged her children tightly to herself for reassurance.

While Ellie distracted the children cutting up some bananas to add to their pancakes, Morgana took her mother to one side and filled her in all that had happened that morning. Delia was extremely indignant on Ellie's behalf that someone would put a body in her business premises, but was unable to think of any explanation for it apart from it perhaps being some madman who had simply come into the first place he'd found to hide it.

"Yes, but he put her in the fridge which is used daily. It's hardly a good hiding place for a body is it?" Morgana pointed out.

"Well no, it's not, but what about the fact that it is very cold in there? Perhaps he thought to make it difficult for the police to estimate a time of death. That could be an important factor you know."

Morgana thought this over. "I think forensics these days are quite capable of compensating for that fact. Wouldn't they just work it out based on the temperature of the fridge?"

"I'm sure I don't know, dear. And if I don't know, then perhaps the murderer didn't know either?"

"I guess so, it sounds plausible." Morgana pondered that and decided her mother had a point, but if the murderer had been trying to use the cold temperatures to disguise the time of death then did that mean that the time of death was relevant somehow? Very probably.

They spent the afternoon strolling along the beach and throwing a ball for a random dog who bounded up to play with the children, but Morgana was aware that Ellie was very quiet. She noticed her sister checking her phone constantly despite the fact there was never any phone reception in Lower Portmage. When they returned to the house, Ellie left another message for Gregory reminding him of her mother's phone number and asking him to ring urgently.

They ate a late Sunday lunch at about 3 o'clock and were just polishing off the last of the beef with roast potatoes and green beans when Delia's home phone began to ring. Ellie sprang to answer it before her mother even had a chance to rise from the table.

"Gregory, thank goodness." Morgana heard the relief in Ellie's voice before her sister lowered her tone, speaking rapidly but quietly, presumably so the children wouldn't hear the conversation. It was ten minutes before she returned to the table, by which time the ice-cream provided the distraction for Ellie to be able to share her conversation.

"That was Gregory," she explained rather unnecessarily. "He's on his way home now but he's also had messages on his phone from the police and they asked him to stop by the station in Bodmin first, to see if he can identify the girl."

"Why on earth would Gregory have any idea who she is?" Their mother looked confused.

"I suppose it's because he is the owner of the business where she was found, so I guess it makes sense that they think he might know? They have no idea so far, apparently," Ellie said, looking somewhat calmer now she'd spoken to Gregory. "He's going to collect the children and me from here later, if that's okay with you mum?"

"Yes, of course, darling. How about we settle the children in front of the television until then with a nice film? How long do you think he'll be?"

"Oh, not much more than two hours I should think. He was already in Taunton when he rang. He said he's spent the morning in a cellar dealing with a broken furnace at one of his Bristol bakeries. There was no reception down there, so he switched the phone off. He'd only just remembered to turn it on again to let me know he was coming and found all our messages. Anyway a film sounds perfect, thanks."

They all relaxed together on the large squashy sofas in Delia's family room and watched an animated children's film, which Morgana suspected the grown-ups rather enjoyed too. It wasn't long before little Martha was fast asleep with her head in Morgana's lap. She stroked the girl's hair and hoped that her niece would never have to see a dead body. She hadn't really realised until that moment quite how shocking it was to have seen the corpse of a strangled girl. Somehow it had not seemed real at the time. It was more like being part of the staged show, or perhaps she'd just watched too many murder mystery dramas on television. But in real life, of course, no one gathered a room full of suspects and pointed to the murderer within a few hours. No, it would be done by the police. Probably a simple case of finding out who the girl really was to discover who had most likely murdered her. The credits were just rolling on the film when the phone rang again, and this time Delia rose to answer it. She was back a moment later.

"Ellie, it's Gregory again for you," she said quietly, so as not to wake the sleeping Martha. Ellie shifted her older children off her and slipped into the other room to take the phone call.

It was the sound of Ellie sobbing in the kitchen that had Morgana quickly, but gently, sliding the small girl onto the cushions beside her and rushing in to see what was wrong. Her mother took a moment longer, making sure that the eldest two children were fully engaged with a new film before following her in.

"What is it? What happened?" Morgana put her arms around her sobbing sister.

"It's Gregory, he's… He's being held overnight for questioning!"

"What? Why?"

"He knew her. The police showed him a photograph and he identified the girl." Ellie gave a few more hiccupping sobs. "She… She used to be his secretary."

Morgana sat down with Ellie at the kitchen table, shock written all over her face.

"But you didn't recognise her? You said you'd never seen her before?"

Ellie shook her head. "I hadn't, it was before we met when he lived in Bristol."

"Oh," comprehension dawned for Morgana. "She's from Bristol, and he was in Bristol last night. Yes, of course. But why on earth would he bring her body back here and put it in the bakery fridge then drive back to Bristol?" Morgana gave a puzzled frown, but Ellie just shook her head again.

"Seriously though, that makes no sense unless they thought he'd meant to hide the body temporarily and intended to move her before you came to work but then he got interrupted? Or perhaps they thought you were in on it too?" Morgana mused.

"For goodness sake, Morgana, that kind of speculation isn't at all helpful! Of course it's not Gregory, he wouldn't do something like this." Delia said, sitting down on the other side of Ellie and putting her hand over her daughters shaking one. "It's clearly some huge mistake. I don't expect Gregory has even seen that girl in years."

So far as we know, Morgana thought, but she didn't voice it. Instead she said reasonably, "But you can see the police's logic. Gregory is the only obvious connection between this girl and the bakery."

Ellie began to cry even harder at these words and

Morgana decided she better shut her mouth before she said anything else make the situation worse.

"Calm down, Elaine," her mother instructed, as Ellie continued to sob noisily, her head now dropping onto her folded arms against the table.

Delia tutted and fetched a glass out of one of the cupboards. Morgana expected her to fill it with water, but instead she moved over to another cupboard and extracted a bottle of brandy. She poured a hefty measure and put it down in front of Ellie.

"Here drink this," Delia commanded.

Ellie pushed the glass away crying too hard to voice her refusal.

"That'll knock her right out," Morgana commented. "Ellie doesn't really drink alcohol."

"That's the point," Delia said with exasperation. "It's what she needs right now."

Morgana nodded with comprehension. "Mum's right, Ellie, get it down you. It will definitely help you chill a bit."

"The children, I need to take care of the children," Ellie managed to protest.

"And I need to take care of *my* children," said Delia. "You and the kids must stay here. Now, drink this and then you'd better go for a lie down. Morgana and I will see to their dinner, don't you worry about it. If we hear from Gregory, we'll wake you immediately. Until then, there is nothing you can do except rest."

"I couldn't possibly rest!" Ellie wailed. But when Delia tipped the glass up to her lips, she took it and drank like an obedient child. Within minutes she was calm, and five minutes after that she rose rather unsteadily to her feet and allowed her mother to lead her to the spare bedroom.

Delia returned to the kitchen. "She'll be out cold in five minutes," she confided in Morgana.

Two hours later and the children were also in bed. Morgana and Delia had just begun clearing up when the back door burst open and Morgana's double appeared, striking an *'I've arrived!'* pose in the doorway.

"Oh joy," Morgana said dryly, eyeing her twin sister. She raised her voice slightly to call out, "Mum, look what the cat's dragged in."

"But I don't have a ... oh! Morwenna, darling. What a lovely surprise!"

"Hardly a surprise, Mother. I sent you an email yesterday about picking me up at the station this evening. I waited an hour and then got a taxi. Did you forget?" Morwenna embraced her mother warmly, apparently unbothered by the lack of pick up.

"I'm so sorry, darling. I didn't forget, I simply didn't see the email. I can't remember my password; I haven't been able to check my messages for weeks."

"Typical mum." Morwenna rolled her eyes. "Isn't your password just 'password'?"

Delia snapped her fingers. "Of course, that's the one. I wonder if I've missed anything important?"

Morwenna exchanged a look with Morgana, who gave a grudging smile of shared acknowledgment of their mother's shortcomings.

"Only your baby girl coming to stay with you." Morwenna gestured to the two bags of luggage at her feet.

"That would be marvellous news at any other time,

it's just…" Delia trailed off helplessly and looked to Morgana.

"Ellie and the children are staying here tonight, and maybe for a few days. It rather depends. Gregory is being held by the police for murder, you see," Morgana supplied.

Morwenna gave a spurt of disbelieving laughter at the statement.

"Morwenna!" her mother chided, shocked by the reaction.

"I'm so sorry, totally inappropriate of me," Morwenna flapped her hands apologetically. "It's just such a surprise. I mean, *Gregory*? Seriously? He's such a dull man to be mixed up in something as sordid as murder."

"I think you mean nice, dear, not dull. That's no way to talk about your sister's husband."

"Very well," Morwenna amended, "nice then. But honestly, who would seriously consider Gregory a murderer? That's crazy."

"Yes," Morgana agreed, "unfortunately it turns out that the murdered girl was his old secretary and her body was found in the fridge of his bakery here in Portmage."

"No way!" Morwenna looked indecently thrilled by this piece of information.

Morgana sighed, but continued with the story knowing that Morwenna would keep asking until she had all the details.

"Gregory has been in Bristol this weekend," Morgana explained, "and this girl lives in Bristol. The only thing connecting her to Portmage is Gregory, hence why the police have arrested him; but *obviously* it wasn't him.

Anyone could have done it. After all, it would be perfectly easy to drive here and then back to Bristol. It's only about two hours each way so you could make a round trip during the night and no one would be any the wiser."

"Yes, but I still can't get my head around how they could think Gregory would do that. Surely bringing her here just incriminates him? He might be dull, but he's not stupid."

"Incriminating him might be the entire point," Morgana said.

Morwenna threw her hands up dramatically. "But why? I mean, he's not exactly the type to inspire enemies is he?"

"Unlike you, you mean?" Morgana gave her sister a sour look.

"Yes, exactly. Interesting people attract other interesting people into their life, like murderers for example. But it's far too exciting an event for an old stick like Gregory."

"He isn't exactly old though, only thirty-five," pointed out Delia.

"No, I suppose not, he just seems older to me. It probably comes from him being married and having three children already. Most men of his age haven't even reached the midlife crisis stage, have they?" Morwenna's eyes twinkled suddenly, "You don't suppose that's what it is, do you?"

"That's enough, Morwenna," Delia said sharply and Morwenna gave a shrug but lapsed into silence. "The immediate problem is that with Ellie and the children here, there's no room for you to stay. You shall have to go home with Morgana tonight."

"What? No way," Morgana protested.

Her mother gave her a firm, "Don't be silly, dear, you have a spare room and mine are all full. Don't fuss Morgana, she is your sister and we take care of family. Besides, the two of you shared a room for nearly eighteen years. A few nights in adjoining bedrooms isn't going to kill you."

"So you say. But if there's another dead body in the morning, it was Morwenna that did me in!"

Chapter Five

Morwenna flopped down on Morgana's couch and stroked the cat who'd come to investigate who she was. "He's a handsome devil, isn't he? What's his name?"

"Lancelot."

"I should have known. You always loved him the most," she laughed and kicked off her high heels. "Good job you drove down to mum's. There's no way I'd have managed the hill in these shoes."

"Yes, not to mention your suitcases. Just how long are you intending to be here?" Morgana eyed the two massive cases she'd just lugged to the doorway of her spare bedroom.

"Oh, they're filled with costumes, barely any real clothes at all. I shall have to borrow some of yours. As to how long, who knows, I'm 'resting', it's an acting term."

"I know what it means," Morgana gave a smirk. "It means you're between jobs and you have no work right now. Why don't you just magically make some leading lady trip on her face, isn't that what you did once before?"

"Only the one time, and the role was supposed to be mine, but she seduced the director, it was deserved." Morwenna waved an airy hand. "Ralston will call me with details of my next role as soon as he's got contracts in place. I'm hardly a jobbing actress, darling. I just turned down several offers so I'm fortunate enough to be able to pick and choose."

"Couldn't you have stayed in London while you picked and chose?"

Morwenna looked dramatically hurt by the comment. "I've come to spend time with my family."

"Humph, well, keep out of my shoe closet," Morgana grouched, feeling guilty for being so unwelcoming.

"Why on earth would I want to step into your shoes, Mog? You work in a shop." Morwenna gave a tinkling laugh and Morgana stopped feeling remotely guilty.

"Don't call me Mog, *Mew*," she sniped back. But Morwenna just grinned at the resurrection of the old bickering and Morgana gave in with a sigh. "Are you hungry?"

"Famished, but then I always am, being permanently hungry is a hazard of my profession. You know, you should probably lay off the cream teas if you want to continue to look just like me. I think your bottom is expanding."

"It is not," Morgana said through gritted teeth, "but looking identical to you isn't exactly high on my wish list. You should have kept the red highlights in your hair, it made you look more individual."

Morwenna ran a hand through her long thick hair. "Too much upkeep, plus my natural colour is a decent shade, a reporter recently described it as dark molasses which sounds rather attractive doesn't it?"

"Yes, except it's *my* hair colour, you were always the one experimenting with the rest of the rainbow. I liked the fact that boyfriends could easily tell us apart."

Morwenna laughed. "You've still never gotten over Tristan Treharne surprising you under the mistletoe and kissing your socks off when he thought you were me. I didn't know if you were going to black his eye or let him carry on."

Morgana flushed at the memory. Her one and only kiss with bad boy Tristan, and she'd let it go on far longer than she should have before pushing him away and icily informing him he had the wrong sister. She sat up suddenly as she realised that Morwenna didn't know that he was the Detective Sergeant on the scene that morning.

"Come on, I'll make us a healthy supper and fill you in on all the action from today. You'll never guess who responded to Ellie's 999 call."

It turned into a nice evening, and the girls shared a bottle of wine and talked until late, managing not to fight for once.

The following morning Morgana had to drag herself out of bed to open the shop, stopping first to ring and check on Ellie.

"She's a bit of a mess," Delia whispered down the phone line. "But she has no doubt at all that Gregory is innocent, and I don't think the police are allowed to hold him for much longer unless they get some concrete evidence. So, we're just going to sit tight today and wait and see."

"Good idea. Do you need me at all? Or Morwenna?"

"No, it would probably help if you kept Morwenna with you. You know how tactless she can be, and I don't think Ellie is up to hearing it right now."

"Tactless is one word for it. But fine, she can stay here. I'll try to wander down to the bakery later and see if the police are making any progress with the crime scene. It will probably do Ellie good to get back in there as soon as possible."

Morgana was just sweeping all the energies from the previous day out of her shop door when Morwenna came down, clutching a cup of coffee and looking a bit worse for wear.

"What on earth were we drinking last night? I feel like hell."

"Just wine, I told you to eat more. I'd have thought you'd have higher tolerance in your line of work?" Morgana narrowed her eyes as she took in Morwenna's dress. "Hey, that's one of mine, you witch!"

Morwenna stroked one hand down the purple lace. "Yes, but it looks so much better on me and actually, despite popular misconceptions, we actresses are usually in bed early and don't drink like fish. You can't when you have to perform two shows a day."

"Fine, but that still doesn't mean you can steal my…" Morgana broke off as she watched Morwenna stop to tickle Lancelot under the chin, and the cat leaned into the caress. Lancelot was very picky about who he liked and Morgana was surprised to see him responding with such affection to her generally unpleasant twin sister.

"So, are you going to help out or just mooch around all day?"

"I'm supposed to be *resting*, not playing the part of a disgruntled sales assistant. But so long as you don't expect me to actually wield that cliché of a broom, then I can work a cash till I suppose." Morwenna slid behind the serving counter and began to try on a selection of pendants that hung on one side.

"That's very gracious of you," Morgana said sweetly, "just keep your sticky fingers out of the takings, okay? If my books don't balance, then I'm going to raise a tornado to ruin your next play."

Morwenna laughed. "You *wish* you had that kind of magic. I'm the only one of us that could actually pull it off." She sipped her coffee and looked thoughtful. "Is Ellie still pretending she's normal?"

Morgana swept the broom more vigorously, annoyed by her sister's boasting. "Yes, for the most part. I haven't seen her do any magic, but then again, it's not possible to *see* what Ellie can do, is it? Not unless she's brewing. I suspect she adds a little to her baking, there's no way her jams are that naturally moreish."

"And how about you? Are you still reading people?" Morwenna looked interested.

"Actually no. I keep my third eye closed most of the time. Ever since discovering the truth about Ryan I've preferred blissful ignorance. I do occasional fortune telling as a side-line of the business, but opening myself up is very draining. I'm working on harnessing it to create a focussed blast of energy out rather than in, but I can't do what you can do yet."

Morwenna looked smug, then wistful. "You do get to be open about what you are, though. I'd never land another role if I went around saying I was a witch. Theatre people are terribly superstitious."

Morgana gave a reluctant smile. "It's not like anyone believes me anyway. They think I'm just acting, for the tourists."

"All the worlds a stage, and all the men and women merely players," Morwenna quoted, extending an arm in a sweeping gesture.

Morgana rolled her eyes and went into her stockroom

to collect up some items to restock the shelves. She heard the bell ting as someone entered the shop, but as she was halfway up a stepladder she didn't bother reacting to the sound. Morwenna would see to it and call her if needed.

"Well, *hello* handsome." She heard Morwenna's most sultry voice drift through the doorway to her. Morgana frowned and froze as she strained to listen to who it was.

"Hi, I came to see how you were since your mother rang me about the bakery being closed. Is there any news? Ellie must be devastated." Harry's voice came clearly, though she couldn't see him from where she was.

Morgana was about to call out when she decided to see if there was even the smallest chance he'd notice that it wasn't her out there. She knew it was highly unfair, especially as he *expected* to see her in her own place of business, but curiosity made her keep silent.

"Well, isn't that sweet of you," Morwenna purred, her tone making Morgana's hackles rise. "I feel better already at the sight of you."

Morgana crept to the open doorway just in time to see Morwenna put her hand over Harry's, which was resting on the counter, and lean forward as though waiting to be kissed.

If she *dares!* Morgana thought furiously. But before Morgana could move, Harry pulled his hand away and grinned.

"You must be Morwenna, Ellie told me you might be visiting soon."

"Yes, she is," Morgana emerged from the stock room, beaming at Harry. It hadn't exactly been an intentional test, but he'd passed it with flying colours.

Harry stepped past Morwenna and took Morgana's hand, pulling her toward him and planting a peck on her lips.

Morgana blushed as Harry hadn't ever kissed her before, not even a peck and not even after their date, but he seemed to be making it plain that *she* was the one he was interested in. Morgana wasn't sure they were really at that stage as yet, but the pout on Morwenna's face made it all the sweeter.

"I'm so sorry about Gregory, it's just shocking, and poor Ellie," Harry's voice was compassionate, but Morgana pulled away from him.

"You don't believe he did it, do you?"

"Of course not!" Harry gave a firm shake of his head. "They'll find who really did it at any moment. It's awful that he has to go through this first, but I'm sure the police are just doing their job. You can understand their line of thinking, wasn't she an old flame of his?"

"An old secretary of his, that's not the same at all. There's no motive," Morgana said, defensive of her brother-in-law.

"So far as we know," Morwenna said darkly. "He might have been banging her on the quiet for years."

"There is a time and a place for your type of talk, and this isn't it!" Morgana rounded furiously on her sister.

Morwenna gave an unbothered shrug. "How would you really know? Have you tried to read him recently?"

Morgana shot her sister a speaking look and glanced nervously at Harry. She didn't know him well enough to be open about her abilities, but Morwenna couldn't be expected to know that, not after Harry had acted as though they were already a couple. Thankfully he didn't seem to pick up on the wording Morwenna had used.

"She's right," he said, "No one really knows what another person is capable of."

"I know, I've known him a lot longer than you, Harry, and I live here, Morwenna, I see Gregory all the time. He's just not a killer."

"Any one of us is a killer in the right circumstances," Morwenna disagreed, unperturbed by Morgana's expression. "It could even have been Ellie. She's *oh so calm* and kind, but if you cross her then she's got her vicious streak. Remember the time she made all your hair fall out after you bent the wheel on her new bicycle?"

"She was thirteen and very hormonal at the time," Morgana said, her eyes desperately trying to tell her sister to shut up.

"She made your hair fall out?" Harry blinked in disbelief.

"Well, yes. She put something in my juice, but it grew back quite quickly."

"It was *something* alright," Morwenna muttered, but she didn't elaborate. It had been one of Ellie's first potions and more effective than even she had anticipated, and she'd been extremely sorry afterwards. Not that it had been much comfort to an eight-year-old Morgana, who'd had to wear a hat to school for a month to hide her baldness.

"You don't seriously think Ellie might have had anything to do with the murder though, do you?" Harry looked between them, unsure of what was being left unsaid.

"No," both women said in unison, both equally sure of Ellie's innocence. But Morgana knew that Morwenna still held misgivings about Gregory. If one of his own family felt that way, even though they were only family by marriage, then the police were sure to doubt his character too. Morgana really hoped Gregory could provide some proof of being elsewhere, otherwise it didn't bode well at all!

Chapter Six

"So that's your latest boyfriend?" Morwenna teased when Harry had gone.

"Not really, we've only been out once," Morgana hedged.

"I'll take him if you don't want him, he'd certainly stave off the boredom of being back home. A little on the short side for me, but those buns looked tight, and biceps to die for. Does he lift weights?"

"It's probably from kneading dough since he's a baker. No, that's not quite right, he's a professionally trained Pâtissier, definitely not your type."

Morwenna gave a cat like smile. "Darling, with a rear like his, he's every girl's type."

Morgana gathered her mental energy, pulling it from inside herself, and then reached out and gave Morwenna a jolt like an electric shot in the arm.

Morwenna yelped with surprise then started laughing. "I'm kidding, Mog. And well done on the power surge, I'm impressed."

There was a long moment where Morgana continued to mutinously glare at her sister, but it took too much effort to stay angry. Plus, she didn't like being bad tempered. It filled the shop with negative vibes and that wasn't good for business. She rolled her shoulders and let her angry energy drain away. There were real customers coming in the door and she needed her smile in place.

Two hours of unenthusiastic helpfulness later, Morwenna seemed to have had enough of retail. She went off on an early lunch break and didn't come back.

The afternoon was quiet, except for Lancelot spotting his arch nemesis and toppling half the window display.

The cat had an ongoing war with a Golden Retriever, and seemed to wait in the window for the dog to pass by. The Retriever would spot Lancelot and start barking, whereupon Lancelot would leap about lashing his tail which would expand to the size of a bottle brush. It was a daily annoyance to Morgana, as Lancelot invariably knocked things down as he taunted the poor dog from behind the safety of the glass windowpanes.

It was finally closing time when the phone rang again and Morgana rushed to answer it, hoping for some news.

This time it was Ellie herself and she sounded desperate. "The police are continuing to hold Greg," she said, tears clouding her voice.

"Can they do that? I thought they had to either charge him or release him?" Morgana frowned at the news.

"That's what I was wondering, apparently they can if they think he's dangerous. But he's not! I don't know what to do, Morgana. Could you speak to them? Maybe use the fact you used to know Tristan to get more information? Or Morwenna could maybe?"

Morgana was highly doubtful that either her or Morwenna's tenuous and years old connection to Tristan Treharne would get him to reveal anything, but she didn't want to say that to Ellie.

"We can but try," she said, trying to sound positive. "At the very least Tristan should be able to explain why the police are continuing to hold Greg. But you'll probably have to resign yourself to the idea that he's not coming home tonight. Have they told you if you can visit him?"

"They said no," Ellie's voice caught. "He can't speak to me while he's *assisting them with their enquiries.* It's so ridiculous."

"Okay, I'll call and annoy them to the best of my ability. You should stay at mum's for the time being."

"I will, but please can you try to find out how long it will be?"

"Of course," Morgana promised. She took a breath while she pondered how to ask a more tricky question. "Ellie, yesterday Tristan mentioned the broken window and then he asked you whether you knew of anyone who might have a grudge, and both times you sort of hesitated. Is there anything you can tell me that you didn't want to tell him?"

There was a long pause on the line, then Ellie said, "It's probably nothing."

"What is?" Morgana prompted.

"It's just that I'm not sure that the murderer came in through the window. You see it was already broken from a previous intruder, only I didn't want to say that because then it would mean a key was used. And there's only four of us that have keys. And now they're focussing on Gregory, I can't say so because it would only incriminate Gregory even more if they thought the murderer had used a key to get in."

Morgana turned the logic over in her mind. "Sure, that makes sense, but just because the window has been broken before it doesn't mean they *didn't* come in that way."

"That's true," Ellie sounded relieved. "But isn't it more likely they came in the door? There's no sign on the outside of the window that the catch is broken."

"I understand you not wanting to incriminate Gregory more, but Ellie, you withheld information from the police in a murder investigation! Don't you understand that makes *you* look guilty, or at the very least you might have broken some law by not saying anything."

"I didn't think of that," Ellie's voice was very small. "I can't change my story now, Mog, it will definitely look like I'm covering something, and I could get into trouble. Don't you think the children are scared enough without me being taken in for questioning too? They know something's wrong; Daniel has been really badly behaved all day."

"But the fact someone broke in before could definitely be relevant. *Why* didn't you mention the previous intruder? I don't remember that happening, was anything stolen? Surely you reported it to the police at the time?"

"Um, no, actually I didn't. Basically because I dealt with it myself. I'd gone back late one night last month, because I was convinced I hadn't switched off the coffee machine. I heard a sound from the kitchen and went in to check it out."

"Ellie!" Morgana said, exasperated at her sister so blithely putting herself in danger.

"Well, it could have been a rat or something awful like that. I didn't think it would be an actual person, not here in Portmage. We don't really get much crime, do we? But I caught the thief red-handed as he was trying to get away with the cash box, which I just stick in a cupboard."

"Good grief! What happened?" Morgana felt apprehension prickle at her.

"I gave him a jolly good talking to."

"You gave him a …? Ellie, are you saying you *knew* the thief?" Morgana calmed slightly.

"Yes, and that's why it was all a bit awkward, you see, with it being Tristan Treharne who was asking. The thief was his younger brother, Bradley."

Morgana blew out a breath and tapped her fingers on the top of her wooden serving counter, thinking about Bradley Treharne. He was probably only seventeen or eighteen and showing every sign of following in his big brother's bad boy footsteps. But a troubled teen wasn't very likely to be in any way connected to the murderer.

"Bradley. Hmm, okay, I can see why you didn't want to mention it to Tristan, but you absolutely must say something about the window already being broken. So, you gave him a talking to? Then he's unlikely to be connected to any of this."

"Actually…" Ellie's voice trailed off and Morgana looked at the phone suspiciously.

"What did you do?" she asked, knowing there was more.

"Well, it's just that he was pretty rude to me. I told him he'd have to pay for the damage, and he refused, and I said I'd tell his mother and he said she would be too drunk to care. Then I felt bad, because what if she isn't looking after him? So, I gave him a box of cupcakes and sent him away with a flea in his ear, but the next day I heard he was laughing about what a soft touch I was and so I might have put a teeny tiny hex on him."

"And he knows?"

"Yes, I did it right to his face. So I guess he could be seeking revenge? He's the only person I could think of when Tristan asked if there was anyone with a grudge against me. I'm not suggesting he's a cold-blooded killer or anything, but what if he came across the body on the cliff or something and decided to put it in my kitchen to punish me back?"

Morgana sighed. "I think you're grasping at straws. How badly did you hex the poor boy?"

Ellie lowered her voice to an embarrassed whisper, "I made him scared of the dark. I know it was dreadful, it's just that I was so angry that he'd do that to my business and then laugh about it. I was being childish."

"If he's scared of the dark then isn't it unlikely that he'd be out at night to find a body?"

"Scared of something isn't the same as not being able to do it," Ellie pointed out. "I just focussed on his most likely childhood fear, but he would still be able to overcome it if he wanted to badly enough."

Morgana tried to picture Tristan's face if she told him that his little brother could have been involved based on the idea that Ellie had hexed him and he was retaliating. She could only imagine the new 'grown up' Tristan being extremely annoyed with her for even suggesting something so ridiculous.

"It's still not feasible, I'm sorry. I think you should be far more concerned about Bradley telling Tristan what happened and Tristan working out that you lied about the window."

"He wouldn't, would he? Surely that would get *him*

into trouble too?" Ellie began to sound really worried. "

"How about if I talk to Bradley? Make sure he doesn't want to cause more trouble?"

"Oh, would you, Mog? That would be fantastic. I know you don't like opening your third eye, just as I don't like throwing around charms and hexes, but if you could just try and see his aura or get a read on him?"

"I don't use my powers for very different reasons to you, but sure, of course I will," Morgana reassured her sister.

"Thank you. I can't have this hanging over me too. I should have just told the truth, but I was thinking of Greg. I didn't consider that it would get me into trouble as well. I can't leave my children without any parents!"

"Calm down, it won't come to that. But you've got to lift the hex now, okay? Otherwise I have nothing to bargain with." She hung up the phone shortly after that and rubbed at her aching head. She felt drained after her long day of work, but she knew Ellie would only panic more and more as she realised what she'd done; so, she put on her coat and set off to visit Bradley Treharne.

She walked down the High Street heading inland. Most of the parts of the village that had a sea view were taken by hotels and other businesses, so the residential area was tucked away in a more sheltered place where the tourists didn't bother to go.

Morgana wasn't sure of Bradley's exact address but she knew roughly where he lived. A small housing estate for those on low incomes. She had sort of followed Tristan there once, not like stalking or anything, well, not exactly. She'd only been fourteen at the time, so it didn't count.

She reached an area where twenty or so houses were clustered, all identical red brick box shapes and felt lost until she spotted a kid fixing his bike.

"Hi, do you know which house Bradley Treharne lives in?"

The kid gave her an up and down look, then clearly decided to be helpful rather than rude.

"Yeah, number six, yeah?" he said, his strong local accent making Morgana smile. She hardly seemed to hear it much these days, just serving the 'grockels'; which was the Cornish term for tourists.

"Um, yeah. I mean, yes. Thank you." Her lip twitched at a sudden memory of her father telling her: *"You'll never be a presenter for the BBC if you can't speak properly."* He'd tried to stop them adopting the local accent as children, preferring that they speak 'The Queen's English'. It didn't seem to matter that none of them actually *wanted* to be a presenter for the BBC. Of course, regional accents were now the direction that the BBC preferred, so he could have a good spin in his grave over that one Morgana mused to herself. Not that he had a grave, having been lost at sea while manning the local lifeboat and trying to save others during a massive storm twelve years earlier.

Morgana stopped outside number six of a street simply called The Close, and eyed the house with misgivings. She'd never met Tristan's mother, but was she really a drunk as Bradley had suggested? Would she be one of those chain smoking wrecks who'd yell at Morgana to get off her property? She really hoped not as she wasn't in the mood for being chastised after eight hours on her feet being perky to customers.

She knocked loudly on the door until a female voice yelled, "It's open," and she let herself inside.

The hallway that greeted her was immaculately clean and hung with photos in frames. Morgana was pleasantly surprised, having expected far worse. She followed the sound of a radio down the hall and into a brightly lit kitchen. Again, it was clean and tidy and the woman who stood at the stove looked charming. Despite the fact that she was wearing a turquoise blue tracksuit and bunny slippers, she'd paired the outfit with a cute 1950's pink frilly apron, which didn't match it at all but made her look very approachable. Morgana recognised her as someone she'd seen around the village but never really spoken with.

The woman looked up from the saucepan of baked beans she was stirring on the stove and smiled.

"Hello love, are you selling something? You're in the wrong neighbourhood if so." She gave Morgana a confused glance. "You look familiar."

"I'm Morgana Emrys, I own Merlin's Attic, on the High Street?" Morgana offered, pinning a cheerful smile to her face.

The woman nodded with apparent delight, "Oh yeah, I remember you, went out with my Tris for a while."

"No, that was…" Morgana stopped as the woman interrupted her.

"You're one of them witches, ain't ya? You the one what cursed Brad? Not that I mind, see, it keeps him out of trouble, and lord knows he's trouble right now, but then teenagers always are, aren't they? The only problem is, love, he can't do his job properly no more. No need for pizza delivery during the daytime, he's got to be able to do it at night, so I do 'ope you're here to lift the curse? I'm sure he meant no real harm."

"Something like that," Morgana said, pleasantly surprised at being faced with a woman who obviously believed that she was a witch but seemed fine with it. She suddenly remembered where it was that she saw this woman each day. "You own a Golden Retriever, don't you? I've seen you out walking him. I'm afraid my cat makes a point of winding him up."

"Oh, aye, that's right. Black cat, isn't it? Sorry about all the barking, Callie is desperate to chase him."

"Callie?" Morgana couldn't help asking curiously.

Mrs. Treharne gave an awkward smile. "Calpurnia. Daft name I know, it's something about Caesar's wife and how she's above suspicion. She's Tristan's dog, you see, and he's a police officer."

"Makes sense," Morgana said, noting the fact that Tristan was obviously a dog person. "Anyway, it's Bradley I'm here to see. Is there any chance I can talk to him privately?"

The woman gave her a worried look. "I know he has done you wrong, but he's a good boy."

"I'm sure he is."

"Like Tris, they do stupid stuff, but they grow out of it, y'know? Look at Tristan now, he's become a Detective Sergeant, can you imagine? Investigating serious crimes and that. But he still takes time to visit me, checks up on us every single week he does." She looked extremely proud at this comment. "An 'e got me a cleaner and everything," Mrs. Treharne added smugly.

"How nice for you, that must be a great help," Morgana said politely. Privately laughing to herself at the mental image of the *old* Tristan interviewing cleaners. The new Tristan sounded too good to be true.

"Turned out right, he did. A boy who looks out for his mother is worth having, mark my words. He could use a good woman though." Mrs. Treharne gave a calculating once over of Morgana and she blushed slightly at the insinuation. Still, it was interesting that he was single. Morgana decided that any comment she made on the subject would probably only encourage the woman to chat, or worse to start matchmaking, so she kept her mouth shut. After a long silence where they both seemed to be waiting, the woman sighed and jerked her head towards the door at the far end of the kitchen. "He's out the back."

"Thank you." Morgana walked to the indicated door, thinking about how easy it would be to misjudge Mrs. Treharne. She could cast a judgement based on where the woman lived, or the fact that her teenage son had claimed that she was a drunk, but she could also take her at face value as a woman who was incredibly proud of her older son for bettering himself and trying her best to be a good mother when she was clearly raising a difficult second son all alone.

In the past Morgana could have looked on Mrs. Treharne using her third eye, and even if she hadn't opened her sight, she would still have perceived the aura of the woman and been able to see in an instant what kind of person she was, but she couldn't do it anymore, and she regretted that now.

Wouldn't it be easy to solve a murder if you could see at a glance who was good and who was evil? Would she ever be able to get that ability back?

Chapter Seven

When Morgana was a child, she'd been able to see auras. It wasn't a perfect way to judge character as it meant that she only saw a snapshot of how that person was at that particular moment. But her abilities had gone beyond that as she'd reached her teens.

She'd also been empathic to their emotions. Great waves of emotions had hit her at times; happiness, contentment and pleasure, but also anger, fear and sadness. She'd already been trying to distance herself and built up defences against it when her father had died and it had become too much.

Surrounded each day by the crushing grief of her mother and her siblings, Morgana had felt it several times over and above as she added theirs to her own.

That was when she'd taken steps to properly suppress her power. She'd found ways through meditation and focus to turn it down, right down until she could hardly see or feel any of it. And, bit by bit, the ability had left her.

She still had occasional flashes, like when someone with an especially strong personality was around, but that had been it. Right up until six months ago when someone she'd trusted had turned out to be a murderer. That's when she realised that maybe she needed those powers. Not like before, but if she had been able to turn them off then surely she could turn them on again when needed? But that had proved very tricky.

She still had her 'third eye' for emergencies, but it was more of a handicap than a help in many situations. It made her physically very weak and unable to regain her real sight for several minutes. She just needed to keep working on switching back on her ability to 'read' people, and to be able to do it at will rather than all of the time.

But now, she had to try to get a sense of Bradley, and she didn't need her magical powers to know that he was going to be difficult.

She took a deep breath, fixed her cheerful smile back in place, and went towards the moody looking young man cleaning a motorbike on the grass.

"So that's what happened to it," she muttered to herself, giving the motorbike a fond look. This was the bike that had caused untold damage to the school playing field after Tristan had decided to do some stunts on the newly laid turf, and the same bike that had caused hearts to beat faster as they heard it approaching. It looked as though Tristan had passed it down to Bradley and she wondered if Bradley managed to pull off the whole image as well as Tristan had.

Bradley looked up and scowled furiously, and Morgana had to restrain herself from laughing at him. Maybe it was her age now, but there was no way this boy had an ounce of that sense of danger that made had once made Tristan so attractive.

She tried to look serious as she regarded him. "Hello, Bradley. I was wondering if we could have a chat about you breaking into the bakery?"

Morgana watched as anger and fear both flickered in the boy's eyes. "Are you here to gloat?" He demanded, shifting away slightly. "Your sister is a total cow."

Morgana raised her eyebrows, expressing her disapproval at his choice of words.

He stood up quickly, trying not to appear intimidated. "I didn't even take her money, what did she have to go and ruin my life for?"

"Ruin your life? Is that how you see it? You could have been in serious trouble but she didn't tell anyone, she was trying to protect you."

He looked momentarily scared. "I didn't mean no harm. It was just a broken window and she can afford to get it fixed better than I can. I've seen the car her husband drives, must'ave cost him twenty grand. I make seven quid an hour like, and I can't even do that not now she's put her voodoo on me."

"Magic, not voodoo," Morgana said, slightly distracted as she processed his words. "So, you haven't told anyone about breaking in?"

"No."

"And you'll be more respectful to her?"

"Don't see why I should. Unless she's changed her mind o'course?" He looked hopeful for a second, before reverting to his scowl.

"She will do if you don't say anything about being in the bakery. It's a bit awkward now, because of the dead body. You could both get into trouble because she didn't tell Tristan that it was *you* who broke her window and not the murderer."

His eyes widened. "Murderer?"

Morgana gave him a searching look. "Haven't you heard about the dead girl being found at the bakery on Sunday morning? I'd have thought it was all over the village by now?"

"I haven't been out, can't afford it now." He glared petulantly. "A real live body?"

"A real *dead* body, yes. So, I'm assuming you had nothing to do with it being there. You weren't out on Saturday night?"

His eyes dropped to the grass and his bottom lip stuck out, reminding her of a toddler.

"You *were* out weren't you?" She guessed.

He threw his cleaning rag down at his feet and put his hands on his hips facing her again. "So what if I was? I won't let that witch force me under me own bed. But it was like being in a nightmare, strange shadows reaching for me, cars without lights trying to run me down, heavy breathing coming from nowhere, and the sea thumping and crashin' like it was getting closer and closer. I'd only had a few pints. I was fine in the pub but walkin' home was horrible."

"Cars without headlights?" Morgana's attention was suddenly caught. "Did you actually see the car?"

"It had its lights off," he said as if she was being stupid, but she noticed he'd looked away again.

"Bradley, can you think carefully if you noticed anything about the car? The make or the colour? You obviously know a bit about cars if you're able to guess the value of Gregory's car."

"Why would I tell you even if I could?" His eyes narrowed as he realised she needed something from him.

"Because you want me to tell Ellie to lift the hex she put on you?" Morgana bargained.

He nodded slowly. "It looked white. I can't be sure."

Not Gregory's car then, she thought, her spirits lifting

slightly. His was a dark blue and wouldn't look white even in the moonlight. Then again, Bradley wasn't exactly a reliable witness.

"Big car or small car?" She pressed for more information.

"I dunno."

"What time was this?"

"I dunno, late. I think it might have just been my mind playing tricks, it was dark. Are we done?" He bent and scooped up his cleaning rag, then kicked over a bucket of dirty water beside him so that it drained away in the grass.

Morgana hastily stepped away before the brown liquid reached her shoes. "Yes, thanks for your help."

"And you'll tell that bi...I mean your sister, to take back her spell?"

"Yes. She's a kind person, Brad, she'd have done it already if you'd just been nice," Morgana softened her tone now, "and she gave you cakes even though you'd just broken her window."

He shuffled his feet. "Yeah, okay. Tell her I said sorry."

Morgana gave him an approving nod and patted the bike as she passed, letting herself out the rear gate onto a rough track that ran down the back of the houses.

She was pleased with her efforts, feeling that she'd managed to gain information and read his emotions despite her current lack of real abilities. Of course, she could be completely wrong. He might be an evil genius who had committed murder and then engineered things so he came across as merely a hapless teen, but she didn't think so. If she couldn't train herself to read emotions again, then maybe she could work this out simply by being observant and intelligent about her questions, just as she had been with Bradley.

"It's the small nuances that make a conversation go the way you want it to," she reassured herself, "he won't say anything."

She was so lost in these thoughts that she jumped when someone tapped her on the shoulder.

"Harry!" She smiled at him. "You surprised me."

"That's because you were wandering along in a daydream. What have you been up to? You have a very smug look about you." He grinned back at her.

"Interviewing a suspect."

He furrowed his brow. "A suspect?"

"Okay, not really. It's the murder of that girl. Ellie thought of someone who might have a grudge against her and who possibly put the body there to make her life miserable. But that was just silly." She didn't want to say that the real reason she'd talked to Bradley was to convince him to unwittingly cover up evidence against Gregory and not reveal something that would get Ellie into trouble.

"I see. So, he's not a real suspect?"

Morgana shook her head. "I seriously doubt it. He just isn't capable of it."

"But how do you really know? Aren't there famous murder cases where it turned out to be the cute little girl who butchered her parents for no discernible reason? Sometimes people are just bad inside and hide it well."

"That's a chilling thought. On that basis it could well be you. You have no obvious motive, but maybe you just like strangling strangers and leaving them at your place of work?"

Harry threw back his head and laughed. "Touché, Morgana. Or *you*, perhaps. Would it help if I told you that Ellie checked my references and none of my previous employers mentioned strangled women cropping up in their businesses?" His expression turned serious and he took her hand. "Ellie tells me that you're good at reading people, what do your senses tell you about me?"

Morgana looked down at where his fingers were twining with hers and felt nothing much but a sudden quickening of her pulse at the intimacy of such a seemingly innocent touch. She tried to push her attraction aside to read him.

She could open up her third eye and see him that way, but she refused to do it. Not only because he would think she was seriously weird when she got all faint and half blind, but also because it was too much of an invasion in such a new relationship. If you *knew* someone was good, then the trust wasn't really trust. And trust was a big deal to her.

Instead she worked hard to get a genuine read on him, to pick up vibrations from the physical contact of their hands. It was elusive but she got a few small bursts.

"I can feel that you're a man of passion," her voice sounded far too husky, even to her own ears. "Passion in your work, primarily," she clarified quickly. "You love life and adventure, you have no fear of travel and new places, but you think before you act. Your spirit of adventure and your passion don't rule you."

"Very good," his own voice lowered to match hers. "But love will always overrule even the sanest of heads.

Make men do reckless things." He closed the gap between them and brushed his lips against hers in a brief feather light kiss that made her senses spin.

Chapter Eight

"Have dinner with me," Harry said, not stepping back. Morgana shook her head, but more to try to clear it than anything.

"Oh, I don't know... I've got my sister staying and it's quite a walk to your place and..." She trailed off; aware she was making excuses.

"Okay, not dinner at my place. Let me take you for something to eat now, somewhere in the village? It's still early so just a light meal? I'd love to hear more about your *investigations.*"

"You don't like taking no for an answer, do you?" She smiled at his persuasion. She looked down at her clothes, wondering if it was really 'date' appropriate, but Harry interpreted her thought and dismissed it.

"You look lovely, as always. Aren't you even a little hungry? It will be quiet in the pub right now and I saw on the specials board that they were doing a clam chowder. Not the easiest dish to master, but I'll bet the clams are fresh off the boats this morning and it doesn't get much better than that does it? Jewels of the ocean, with bacon, garlic, shallots and new season baby potatoes, all wallowing in a rich double cream and butter sauce, and perhaps a hint of thyme?"

"The way you talk about food makes it completely irresistible," Morgana capitulated, "though I suspect you know that only too well. I just hope the chowder lives up to your expectations of it." She thought briefly of

Morwenna, possibly waiting for Morgana to cook her something, and decided that she'd much rather go to the pub with Harry. Morwenna was resourceful, she could take care of herself perfectly well. She sent her sister a quick text message and then gestured to Harry to lead the way.

Together they strolled back to the High Street and entered the charming warmth of the pub. The restaurant area was filled with enticing smells coming from the kitchen and their table by the back window gave them a view of the sun starting to set over the sea.

"So, I hear your family have lived here for generations?" Harry said, once they were settled.

Morgana shook her head. "Not always. Quite often they've left Portmage and moved to other places, even to other parts of the world. But yes, we can trace bits of our family line here all the way to the dark ages because they always seem to come back, usually within a generation or so." She smiled to herself since it seemed as though so many of her ancestors had tried to leave but something had always made them return, something magical she suspected.

"It sounds like there's a story there?" Harry regarded her curiously.

Morgana leaned back in her chair, "It's a long story, a very, very long story, full of myths and legends and magic and murder."

"Now I'm officially interested, I do like a good murder." He grinned at her.

"Perhaps some other time," she said, not ready to share her entire family history with him so soon, especially as so much of it was tied up with the whole witchcraft thing and she had no idea how he felt about that yet.

"I have a question for you," she said, changing the direction of the conversation. "How did you know that Morwenna wasn't me?"

Harry laughed. "I'd like to say that I sensed it, that I just somehow knew. But that wouldn't be telling the truth." He reached forward to tap the charm bracelet on her wrist. "It was this, I've never seen you without it. When I came into the shop and you flirted with me, or at least what I thought was you flirting, it made me pause for a second. It just wasn't like you, and some instinct made me check your wrist. When I saw that she wasn't wearing the bracelet, it was an easy guess."

Morgana raised her brows, "That's still a very impressive deduction. I like it that you noticed that." She favoured him with a warm smile, and her hand closed around his.

"I assume your twin sister is here now to comfort Ellie?"

"Not so as you'd notice," Morgana said, "It was just a coincidence that she came yesterday."

"Still, I'm sure Ellie is grateful to have her family around her. They're still holding Gregory, aren't they?"

"Are you starting to think maybe he did it?" She withdrew her hand. "I thought you believed in him."

He gave a rueful grimace. "I don't mean to throw accusations. Greg is absolutely not a killer. It's just… Well, it looks pretty bad, doesn't it? He's the only connection between that girl and Portmage, and you said he was in Bristol on Saturday night, and she lives in Bristol…" he trailed off as Morgana's expression darkened further.

She glared for a moment and then gave a sigh of acceptance. "It does sound bad when you put it together. But there's still the small thing called motive. He had no reason, and before you run with Morwenna's suggestion that they were having an affair, I can tell you that it's jolly unlikely. He and Ellie are happy! He's never shown interest in anyone else."

"Maybe the girl was the one chasing him?" Harry suggested. "Maybe she made a pass at him and then threatened to tell Ellie it was more than it actually was? Perhaps he killed her to keep her quiet, that could be a motive, to protect Ellie?" He gave a shrug to show he was just throwing ideas.

"Maybe," Morgana was unconvinced. She wanted to reiterate that Gregory just wasn't the type. But how well could she really trust her own judgement? She didn't actually see Gregory all that often and so it was difficult to be a hundred percent sure. And he did work away a lot, usually back in Bristol maintaining his businesses there.

"This is making you uncomfortable," Harry said, taking her hand again and squeezing it. "Let's move on to a more cheerful subject. You were going to tell me about some of the good surfing spots in the area?"

Morgana relaxed slightly. "You're right; casting suspicions on Gregory just feels wrong, even though I see the logic behind what you're saying. So, surfing is a great topic. Sea air, the water, the waves, the distant horizon, that's hard to beat, right? I used to surf a lot as a teenager, though I don't really do it anymore." She was distracted as her thoughts drifted to hot summer days and hot sandy guys with 'surfer' hair. "Where have you already been so far?"

"Well, obviously I live down on Pixie Cove and that has pretty good surf, especially with the high spring tides, but I wanted to try a few different beaches. Fistral Bay is an obvious spot for some good waves, and that's where I was on Sunday. As it was my day off, I got up really early and headed off, which was why I didn't get back to Portmage until late on Sunday night and why I totally missed the news about the dead girl in the bakery until Monday. I've also been to Polzeath, but the waves were pretty tame."

Morgana nodded in agreement. "Yeah, it's quite messy surf too, though good for body boarding and beginners. There are a few other obvious ones, which I'm sure you've looked up online? Woolacombe, Bude and Croyd to the north of here, and then Perranporth, Praa Sands and Sennen Beach in the south. But there are a few hidden bays that only the locals know about. There's a fantastic one just on the other side of Portmage from where you are. It's called Witch Haven Beach and you can only access it from the sea. You need to paddle round the cliffs from Lower Portmage, but you have to be really careful, especially at this time of year. It's best to look up the times of the tides before you try it. There's a rip tide around the spring and autumn equinox that should never be underestimated."

He looked serious as he considered her words. "I'm not sure I'm experienced enough yet for that."

"Really? I thought you were a regular surfer. Ellie said you moved here for it?"

He pushed his hair off his face with a rueful grin.

"Enthusiasm and ability are not remotely the same thing. I love to surf, but it doesn't mean I'm any good at it."

She laughed. Harry just didn't seem like the kind of person who'd be bad at anything. She was sure he would quickly become competent at any skill he turned his attention to.

Their food arrived and they talked and ate, and Morgana found herself becoming more and more inclined to throw caution to the wind. She thought she might spend the entire night with Harry, if he asked her to, of course.

"Are you sure I can't tempt you to a real drink?" Harry said persuasively as Morgana topped up her water glass.

"I really shouldn't, I have to work tomorrow and it's a nightmare job when you have a hangover."

"One sherry won't give you a hangover, and it would go excellently with tiramisu." He nodded his head to the nearest table, and Morgana looked over just in time to see a man offering his date a forkful of tiramisu. Her mouth watered slightly at how good it looked. She was just about to capitulate when her phone began to ring. She gave Harry an apologetic look and retrieved the phone from her handbag.

"Mum? Everything okay? Is there news?"

"I'm sorry to call so late," Delia said, sounding worried. "It's just that Ellie took the bus over to Westpoint Station this afternoon to demand to speak with Greg, and she's just called in a total state. They've been questioning her and treating her like she's the murderer and she doesn't feel up to making her own way home. I can't drive there because I have the children and

I've already put them to bed."

"Do you want me to go and get her?" Morgana offered immediately.

"Would you, darling? I'd be so grateful."

"Of course, I'll set off in a few minutes."

She grimaced at Harry, genuinely regretful to end their evening so abruptly. "I'm sorry about dessert, but duty calls."

He waved a hand dismissively. "Family first, we can do dessert any time." He gave her a lingering look of promise that made her think he'd been well aware of how close he'd come to getting very lucky.

"Maybe we'll start with dessert next time," she said, her voice coming out more sultry than she'd meant it to.

"I'd like that."

Morgana reached into her bag for her wallet, but Harry shook his head. "I invited you. Now go, it's a twenty-minute drive and it sounds as though Ellie needs you sooner rather than later."

"Thank you. I guess it's just as well I didn't drink. Next time, I'll make sure I have nowhere I need to be." She rose and he stood up too. On impulse, she leaned forward and kissed him opening her senses to see if she could glean whether he was hiding any annoyance at the interruption.

Her powers might be pretty rusty, but physical contact helped a lot.

There was no hint of annoyance, instead it was something unexpected... *relief?*

His relief could be taken as a bad sign, but even though the kiss was brief, she could feel the chemistry spark instantly between them. She could tell he wanted to take more, yet was holding back.

Morgana felt exactly the same way.

She left the pub, pleased with the experiment. It had shown her she was right about the attraction; it was very much mutual between the two of them. What she had felt in the kiss had clear potential to spark into something much more passionate. Morgana spent the drive to Westpoint Police Station reliving that moment. She remembered the way his lips parted very slightly against hers. The way they felt, the way they moved, even the brief hint of stubble on his face. She wondered if he, too, had closed his eyes at that moment. No other part of them had been touching, but even the brief contact had been more than enough to heighten all of her senses. She hadn't expected to find herself longing for more, especially after what had happened with Ryan.

Ryan had been the biggest mistake of her life, making her fearful for a good while afterwards, especially as she didn't seem able to trust her own intuition anymore. It had been a long time before she felt ready to date anyone else, and she'd only recently allowed herself to try again.

Since then she'd been out twice to dinner with Jamie Fenchurch, who worked as a landscape gardener in the village, and once to a party that Jamie had invited her to. But even after three evenings with him, she hadn't felt the same sort of spark that she'd just experienced in a few short minutes with Harry.

Spending time with Jamie had felt more like an evening with a friend than anything else. She liked Jamie, and they got on well enough, but that elusive quality was missing. He'd just been too... *nice*, for lack of a better word. He was handsome and undoubtedly one of the good guys, which was what she wanted, but if it wasn't there then it just wasn't there.

And with Harry, it was *definitely* there.

She thought about what she felt when she opened her senses. In the old days, her powers would have caused his feelings to constantly bombard her, to wash over her whenever she was near him. But those days were long gone; what had once been a flood of raw emotion was now more like a trickle, drips and drabs that she had to mentally grab a hold of and pin down to examine. It didn't help her much, either, it was only what he had been feeling in the exact moment. Still, she'd managed to get *something*, and that was progress on regaining some of her power.

She thought now about the odd mixture of desire that she'd felt mingled with a sense of relief that she was leaving. She shrugged to herself, supposing that it actually made sense. He had, after all, mentioned an ex-wife. Presumably he'd gotten burned badly in the divorce, and he was probably as fearful as she was about jumping into a new relationship.

In other words, they were two cautious people playing a long game.

Morgana nodded to herself; yes, that suited her very well right now. She could be patient with him, and he would be patient with her. That way, things would have time to properly develop into something else, something more than the feeling of lust she'd been left with after that one single kiss. Morgana was still grinning to herself at the memory as she swung her car into Westpoint police station and found a free parking spot. It was pitch dark outside, but the police station was lit up like a beacon.

Morgana didn't know the officer behind the reception desk. He was a large man in his late forties, and judging by the ruddy look on his face, she was fairly sure he was a heavy drinker. He was obviously on for the evening shift and none too happy about it, judging by the grumpy look he gave her.

She explained that she was there to collect Ellie, and perhaps see Gregory if possible.

"She ain't done yet," the man said. "You can wait over there, shouldn't be more than half an hour or so." He jerked his head towards a row of three uncomfortable looking plastic chairs set against the wall.

Morgana was just going to make her way over when the office door opened to the right of the reception desk and Tristan Treharne's head popped out. "I thought I heard your voice, Morgana."

She inclined her head in greeting. "I've come to get Ellie, and I was wondering if there is any chance of talking with Gregory?"

Tristan looked thoughtful a few seconds and then made a gesture beckoning her into his office. "Come in and wait here. We have some time, the Inspector is still with Ellie at the moment. Just processing paperwork, nothing to worry about too much."

"Okay, thanks." Morgana circled past the reception desk to enter Tristan's office. She smiled when she saw the mess of papers all over his desk. Somehow, with his new smart suits and shorter hair, she'd expected Tristan to have become organised and efficient too. But she was delighted to see the haphazard nature in which he still kept his own space. Several pictures lined a corkboard beside his desk, the body of the girl pinned between photos of Gregory and Ellie. Morgana raised an eyebrow as she caught sight of her sister's picture. "Is Ellie seriously a suspect?"

Tristan shook his head. "No, but she's still a person of interest, and she *does* have a motive. We finally heard back from the Avon and Somerset Constabulary in Bristol who have been into Miss Allsopp's home and found signs of a struggle there. That means she was definitely attacked in Bristol, and then brought here afterwards. While I do think Ellie is quite capable of *physically* managing the task, she doesn't seem like the type of person who would drive off in the middle of the night and leave her three small children alone. At least not based on the short time that I've spent with her," Tristan explained. "I think it's highly doubtful that she's involved in any way at all."

"Well of course not!" Morgana said, sitting down in the chair opposite him as he took the seat behind the desk. "I'm glad you can see that, at least. She is a very good mother and will always put those children first. So, the girl was called Miss Allsopp?"

Tristan nodded. "Yes, we can confirm her identity now, thanks to Mr. Westbrook identifying the body. Kendra Allsopp, aged 28, single."

"But how do you know she's single? It could easily have been a boyfriend, isn't that quite probable?"

"It just means unmarried. The police in Bristol spoke with her previous employer and it does look like there *might* have been a boyfriend, though we haven't been able to find any trace of one. But her employer hadn't seen her for a few months, so it seems likely the relationship had ended. No one has come forward and there is nothing at her home to indicate anyone else having stayed there."

"A few *months?*" Morgana asked curiously. "Why hadn't he seen her in a few months?"

Tristan picked up his pen and began to shuffle through the papers on his desk, pausing after a moment before suddenly looking up at Morgana with narrowed eyes. "Just a minute, are you using some of your mojo on me to get me to tell you details of the case?"

Morgana gave a sputter of laughter. "My *mojo?* What is that, exactly?"

Tristan pursed his lips. "I can't believe I'm saying this in here, at *work* of all places. But you know exactly what I mean. Your *magic*," he whispered the last word, practically hissing it as he spoke.

Morgana gave him a long considering look. "You seem quite sure I have magic?"

"Don't play coy with me, Morgana. I used to go out with Morwenna, remember? I've seen *exactly* what she can do. I know all about how she can move things with her mind and twist up your thoughts."

Morgana gave another laugh, and Tristan looked annoyed. "What? Are you going to try to tell me that it was all some kind of *trick?*" he asked.

Morgana shook her head. "No, sorry. You're quite right that Morwenna can use energy to push objects. However, if she messed with your mind at any point, there was nothing magical about it. I promise you; she doesn't have the power to twist thoughts around—at least not supernaturally. If she did manage to do it, it was by the same power that any other woman would've used.

Just simple feminine wiles, no magic needed. My sister is *excellent* at getting her own way through those means," Morgana explained with a small, wicked smirk. "Why? Did she make you do things you didn't want to do?"

"N-No," Tristan conceded, actually blushing at the reluctant admission. "You're right, I probably wanted to do all the things that she suggested just as much as she did. But she was still a bad influence. Anyway, that's all ancient history now."

Morgana gave him a speculative gaze. "You do seem to have changed quite a bit," she noted.

Tristan pushed the papers on his desk into a rough stack, avoiding meeting her eyes as he spoke. "I've grown up, that's all. It happens." Pausing to clear his throat, Tristan continued in a voice that he obviously hoped would sound casual. "And how is Morwenna these days? Has *she* changed very much?"

"Not in the slightest," Morgana said with a grin, shaking her head. "She's as rebellious as ever I promise, and doing very well for herself regardless. She's home for a few days if you wanted to see her?"

Tristan's head jerked up. "She's *back* in Portmage?"

"Indeed, the prodigal sister returns. Except she's been nothing but a pain so far."

Tristan tapped his pen against the papers. "She hasn't been via Bristol before coming back or anything suspicious like that, has she?"

"Not so far as I know," Morgana glared at him for thinking such a thing. It was absolutely fine for her to think the worst of her sister, but she didn't like it when an outsider did the same.

"No, of course not," Tristan agreed hastily. He shook

his head as though to clear his thoughts. "Though Morwenna always did bring drama wherever she went."

"That she did," Morgana agreed. "And now she's gone and made an entire career out of it. She's an actress now, you know?"

"Oh yes, I had heard. Quite successful, according to the gossip columns."

Morgana's mouth quirked. "You read them?"

"Of course not." But he was looking down at his papers again, and she didn't believe him. She wondered if he still held a candle for Morwenna. Somehow, it was a depressing thought, considering how sensible he'd become in other ways. But then, she supposed, you never did forget the first person to break your heart.

Just as Morgana had never forgotten that Tristan had been her first real kiss.

Chapter Nine

Ellie was tearful when she finally came out. She hadn't been allowed to see Greg, and she'd been asked a lot of questions about their marriage that had upset her. Morgana gave her sister a hug and then ushered her to the car, where Ellie sat and stared out the window in miserable silence.

Morgana didn't push Ellie to speak. Instead, she thought about what she had learned and tried to come up with any kind of plausible explanation for why Gregory might have committed murder, or who else could possibly be a link between him and the girl. There must be people in Bristol who had known both Gregory and Kendra Allsopp. People who might've had a reason to want her dead. It wouldn't have been hard for them to discover where Gregory lived, an easy way to deflect blame onto someone else.

The only trouble was, Morgana simply didn't know enough about Kendra to *find* any of those people. She supposed that the police were looking into the girl's background, including friends, enemies, and any other relations she might've had.

But even so, they weren't motivated in the same way that she was to prove Gregory's innocence. Perhaps when Ellie was ready to talk, she might be able to shed some light on the matter. Better yet, Morgana hoped that soon they'd be able to speak with Gregory directly. As she drove across Bodmin Moor, the darkness stretched away on either side of her, and it occurred to her how very easy it would be to switch off her lights and become effectively invisible.

The distance from Bristol to Portmage could easily be done in a couple of hours, and someone could have come from there and back again by morning before anyone suspected that they'd even gone.

She just wished there were more suspects. At the moment it seemed the investigation was wholly concentrated on Gregory. Wasn't there supposed to be a whole list of potential murderers that she could somehow look at, using her abilities, and find the real killer?

She had seen a murderer with her third eye once before, and now she knew exactly what to look for. Unfortunately, using that power also meant making herself vulnerable. The exhaustion that came with it would've been dangerous enough on its own, but that wasn't the only danger. Being able to see the invisible energies that swirled around all living beings was incredibly useful at times, but it left her as good as blind when it came to perceiving the real world at the same time. Morgana could use her power to find out who people truly were, but it also left her completely at their mercy—far from ideal if she was to confront another murderer.

This time, she would need to be smarter about how she went about it. Perhaps she could sit inside a locked car, checking people without even noticing her presence? At least that way, when she inevitably got overwhelmed with exhaustion and could no longer see, she'd be in a safe space with ample time to recover her senses.

"They know something, the police. Something about Greg that they aren't telling me," Ellie said, breaking the silence.

"Like what?" Morgana gave her sister a worried glance.

"That's the problem, I don't know. It doesn't seem right that they know something about my husband that I don't, but it was so obvious. There was pity in that inspector's eyes. *Pity!*"

"It wasn't Gregory," Morgana said firmly. "Whatever they *think* they have on him, they're wrong."

"How can you be sure? Have you actually seen anything in his aura? Or are your powers still on lock down?" Ellie seemed angry, but Morgana knew it wasn't really directed at her.

"I'm working on it, Ells. I've been trying to get it back since that murder last Halloween, but it isn't easy. Not after all those years of suppressing every hint of psychic sense."

"Try harder, I need to *know.*" Ellie's face moved from anger to fear.

"You already know. It wasn't him." Morgana reached out and briefly covered her sister's hand with her own. She just desperately wished she felt as sure as she sounded. Could she trust her own judgement? She'd been wrong before, and it had nearly cost Morgana her life.

"What were you talking to Tristan Treharne about?" Ellie asked.

"Morwenna mostly."

"Her timing couldn't have been worse, could it?" Ellie

said bitterly. "But that's so like her. Just breeze in and think that the world only revolves around her needs."

"She's been okay actually, so far at least," Morgana said, remembering Morwenna putting in almost an entire two hours helping her out at the shop.

"Right. Until she sees Harry. You do realise she'll take him from you without a second thought, don't you?" Ellie wiped a tear from one eye.

"She can *try*; but it so happens that Harry has already encountered her and knew right away that she wasn't me. He wasn't even fooled by her pretending to be me," Morgana couldn't hide the hint of pride in her voice, that her newest crush had actually knowingly chosen *her*.

Unlike Ryan. The thought came unbidden into her mind. When he'd found out that she had a twin sister, his suggestion regarding the three of them had been less than savoury. At least she had the comfort of knowing Morwenna would have refused too.

Morwenna did *not* share her toys.

"She'll keep trying, you know. She'll see it as a challenge," Ellie warned.

Morgana sighed. "I know. Ever since the night I let Tristan kiss me, she's been looking to get back at me."

"Why *did* you let him kiss you?" Ellie asked curiously. "It's not like you to make out with someone else's boyfriend. I would've thought you'd have slapped his face for trying."

"I *did* push him away," she said, heat rushing to her face. "He thought I was her, that's all."

"I was there, as I'm sure you remember. You didn't exactly push him away *very fast*. I think a full minute passed first," Ellie said, making Morgana feel even worse.

"It was *not* a full minute, it was seconds at most," she gave a groan of guilt. "I just really, *really* liked him; I couldn't help myself. But I was only fifteen, for goodness sake! It's been years now."

"And yet, you still like him even now don't you?" Ellie gave Morgana a teasing look, and Morgana knew her sister was trying to distract herself from falling apart over Gregory. She was all for the distraction, but this was a bit too close to home.

"I *don't*," Morgana protested. "He's not the same person now anyway. Besides, he was Morwenna's boyfriend. That makes him a no-go zone until the end of time, and that's all there is to it."

"And you have Harry now. How's that going, by the way?"

"Good, I think. Enough about men," Morgana said, changing the subject as she didn't really want to discuss Harry just yet. "I assume the children are still at mum's house, do you want me to drop you there? Or, shall we pick them up and I take you all home?"

"I'm going to stay at mum's for now. I can't face going home without Greg."

Morgana bit her lip, hoping that it wouldn't eventually come to that.

They were just pulling into Portmage when Ellie's phone rang.

"Greg? Oh, thank goodness! I miss you so much! Have they released you?" Ellie clutched the phone, shooting a glance at Morgana who understood the look and stopped the car, ready to turn around if necessary.

"What?" Ellie's voice rose shrilly. "I don't understand,

why? Why would they do that?" Ellie paused listening, then turned to Morgana. "They've formally arrested him. He's been charged with murder."

Chapter Ten

Morgana had to drag herself out of bed the following morning. It had been another late night, with driving to Westpoint and then the work involved in settling Ellie back in their mother's house. Understandably, her sister had been inconsolable throughout it all.

Morwenna had been out for the count when Morgana finally made it back home, and she was still sleeping as Morgana went downstairs to open her shop the following morning. Perhaps Morwenna really had been telling the truth that actresses drank very little and went to bed early. Or perhaps her London lifestyle had taken its toll, and she'd returned to Portmage to catch up on her beauty sleep.

Morgana had a busy morning restocking shelves and putting through orders, interrupted only by the occasional browser. It was after lunch when Morwenna finally appeared looking well-rested and with her hair freshly washed. Morgana felt haggard beside her sister.

She filled Morwenna in on the latest developments regarding Gregory's arrest, but Morwenna simply said, "I told you so." She then did a circuit of the shop touching various things and pulling faces at the price tags until she eventually hopped up onto the serving counter and crossed her legs, making herself comfortable.

"I thought you said you weren't going to steal my shoes," Morgana said, glaring at Morwenna's feet.

"You can't seriously think I *wanted* to? These are

perfectly hideous. But none of mine are really suitable for walking around the village, are they?"

"No, they're not," Morgana agreed flatly. "What on earth possessed you to pack six pairs of kitten heels for a visit to Portmage?"

"How *precise* of you," Morwenna said, raising an eyebrow. "I see somebody saw fit to paw through my suitcase?"

"And I see you've been through my drawers, too. That 'resting witch face' t-shirt is definitely mine." She looked suspiciously at the jeans Morwenna also wore and decided they, at least, weren't hers. "Except, I swear that t-shirt doesn't look nearly so tight across the chest on me. Don't tell me you've had your boobs done?"

"Don't be silly, it's just a push up bra."

"It's a pneumatic bra is what it is."

"If you want to borrow anything of *mine,* feel free," Morwenna said, breezily deflecting the argument before it started. "Goodness knows you need an update to your wardrobe. Especially, if you're going to go out for dinner with a handsome man. I take it your late night means it went well? Did he grind your nightshade?"

"Did he what?" Morgana quirked an eyebrow, looking up from her order book.

"Grind your nightshade, pump your pepper, put some gin in your zinger," Morwenna laughed.

Morgana shook her head. "Where do you pick these expressions up? And no, we don't all jump into bed with a man on the first date."

"Boring," Morwenna said in a singsong voice. She then proceeded to rip open a bag of salt and vinegar crisps and eat them noisily as Morgana tried to refocus on her stock ordering.

"Do you mind not dropping crisps all over my floor," Morgana complained. "I just swept that this morning."

"Ah yes, the old morning ritual cleanse, you still do that then? Get out the twiggy broom stick and sweep all the negative energy out the door? How very witchy for someone who doesn't like to use her powers. Anyway, I've already finished the crisps, so stop going on." Morwenna tore open the packet and began to lick the crumbs off the inside, freezing in place as the shop door opened and Tristan walked in.

She stared at him, then gave the crisp bag one last long lick before tossing it over her shoulder, heedless of it landing on the floor behind the counter. Jumping down to the ground, she walked across the shop floor to greet the man. Her movements were almost feline as she made a show of sizing him up, looking every inch the predator as she prowled closer to him.

"Morwenna, still as sexy as ever." He gave her an appreciative up and down in return, making her smile like a cat that got the cream.

"The *infamous* Tristan Treharne," she countered. "Not *quite* the same, shame." She reached up and pushed the fingers of one hand through his now cropped hair.

As Morgana watched the intimate touch, both their auras flared into sight. Sexual energy crackled around them in waves of purple, strong enough to pierce through and be visible to Morgana even without her opening her senses.

It was *not* a spectacle that Morgana particularly wished to see.

"You're right," Tristan said, reaching up to clasp

Morwenna's wrist and pulling her hand down and away from him. "I'm not the same. I learned some lessons the hard way, and one of them was to avoid girls like you. I've actually come to see Morgana, on a work-related matter."

Morwenna gave a dramatic pout. "How unkind. Still, we both know there's unfinished business between us." She moved fast, pressing a kiss to his cheek before he had time to respond then flitted back to the counter. "He's all yours, sister... for now." Morwenna gave Morgana a wink.

Morgana took a deep breath to squash her irritation and gave Tristan a tight smile. "What can I help you with?"

"Is there somewhere we could talk, or is this a bad time?"

Morgana looked at Morwenna. "I don't suppose you'd watch the shop for a while?"

"What's it worth?"

"Gratitude? No? Okay, you can keep the t-shirt."

Morwenna appeared to think for a second and then said, "Fine, go on then."

Morgana beckoned Tristan to follow her upstairs, and they'd just reached the door to her flat when Morwenna's voice floated up to them. "I'd advise keeping your pants on. She's got a raging case of herpes."

Morgana's face flushed a deep red. "I do *not* have herpes!" But Tristan was laughing.

"Ten years and she hasn't changed at all?" he asked.

"If you mean, does she still manipulate, cheat and steal? Then no, she's not changed one bit. But it's not *quite* on the scale that a police officer needs to worry about," she hastened to add.

"You're wrong there, she's done plenty the police have worried about a great deal!" he informed her, pulling out a chair at her kitchen table and sitting down.

"Like what?" she said, full of curiosity as she switched on the kettle to make them both some tea.

He shook his head. "It's not my place to say."

"Useful," she commented wryly. "So, did you secretly come to see her for yourself?"

"No. I came to return the keys for the bakery to Elaine. But given that we've just arrested her husband, I thought it might be more prudent if I returned them to you. We're done processing the scene now."

Morgana nodded. "Thank you. Does that mean you have enough evidence now for your arrest, or is it simply a case of having no other suspects?"

"I'm afraid it's the first, there's a great deal of evidence against him."

"Like what?" Morgana asked, offering Tristan the tea.

Tristan accepted it and stared into the mug, a frown on his face. "I really shouldn't be talking to you about this, even if we are old friends."

"Hardly," Morgana said, watching his face closely. She had certainly never thought of them as friends, but she was flattered that perhaps he did.

"I've always valued your opinion, Morgana. I remember well how perceptive you used to be. You would have made a great detective."

"Is there anything you *can* tell me? I'd really like to help. Gregory is my brother-in-law, but that's not the reason I think he's innocent. I truly don't believe he would have done this. I presume you've looked into the past of the victim in detail?" She sat down opposite him and made an attempt to open her senses as wide as she could, desperate to see if she could learn anything new from Tristan without him having to actually say the words.

But trying to read Tristan's aura was like trying to read a book with a thick blanket wrapped around her head. Morgana's powers simply didn't function properly anymore, and something told her that Tristan would not look kindly on her initiating physical contact just to supernaturally snoop on him.

"Of course we have, and in fact for a while it looked as though we'd found an excellent motive for murder. Miss Allsopp had quite recently inherited a very large sum of money."

"How much is a very large sum?" Morgana asked.

"Millions. She was an only child, and with her mother already deceased when her father died, she was the sole beneficiary."

"So, who will inherit the money now that she is dead?"

"The only other family is a distant cousin, but she lives abroad. We've already enquired as to whether she might have travelled to England recently, but her passport expired years ago. It seems fairly conclusive that she's been safe at home this whole time and hadn't had any contact with Kendra since they were children so the money trail is a bit of a dead end. People usually only commit murder for one of three reasons. It's either money, hate, or love. Kendra doesn't seem to have had any enemies, no one seeking revenge or mad with jealousy. That just leaves love, which brings us back to your brother-in law."

Morgana shook her head decisively. "No way, Greg and Ellie are very happy together. I simply don't believe that he was in love with someone else."

Tristan regarded her thoughtfully, and the moment stretched as he was obviously weighing up what to share. "He was seen with Miss Allsopp on the night she was killed. Phone records indicate that she called his hotel room on Saturday afternoon, and we have video footage from the street camera in central Bristol that shows them going into a bar together and leaving again together. Witnesses say they were arguing, and her time of death is judged to be only about an hour later than when they left the bar. Hotel security footage shows that he didn't return to his room until the early hours. He had the time to kill her and to drive to Portmage and back."

"Oh," Morgana said, processing the new information bleakly. "That does sound pretty grim. But I get the feeling you still have some doubts. Why else would you be here now, talking to me about it?"

Tristan ran a hand through his hair. "I don't know. It's just a gut instinct, I guess. Something doesn't make sense, but I can't see what it is. The evidence points only to Gregory, but if he is actually innocent, it would help me enormously if he would just *talk* to me. That way, maybe I could figure out what's wrong with the picture. But he won't, he just keeps denying everything and then refusing to say another word. It's so frustrating and it only incriminates him further."

"So, you're actually trying to help him? Not trap him into giving you details to build your case against him?"

He gave her a serious look. "We don't try to trap people, Morgana, that's not how this works. Nobody wants to put an innocent man behind bars. I wish people would just work *with* the police rather than against us, but we can't do that if people won't help themselves."

Morgana thought guiltily of Ellie holding back information on her broken window. "Can I see him? Are we allowed to talk to him now?"

"Yes, he's allowed visitors now, under supervision. Do you think you can get him to tell you anything?" Tristan leaned forward and suddenly Morgana could see the anticipation glittering around him. She made another effort to open her senses, but he remained incredibly difficult to read.

"Okay, I expect Ellie will be there this evening, so I'll drive over first thing tomorrow if that's all right, and I'll see if I can get him to tell me anything or at least try and convince him to tell you everything he knows."

"I appreciate that." Tristan rose to his feet, retrieving a set of keys from his pocket along with a piece of paper. "I'll need you to sign for them."

Morgana nodded, signing the paper before putting the keys to Ellie's bakery on a shelf behind her.

"You can go out the back door if you want to, unless of course you'd rather have a lingering goodbye with Morwenna?" she asked, only half teasing him.

"Definitely not," he said with feeling. "I'm on duty, lead us not into temptation and deliver us from evil." Tristan joked.

As Morgana waved him off, the depressing thought crossed her mind that even though she and Morwenna looked identical, nobody had ever considered *her* an evil temptation. Then she went back to the shop to quiz Morwenna about what she might have done to interest the police, and to make sure she hadn't stolen anything

Chapter Eleven

"I told you he was knocking off the secretary," Morwenna pronounced as they settled down for a roaring night of revelry drinking hot chocolate in their pyjamas.

"I don't believe it," Morgana shook her head.

"You're so naïve."

"And you think the worst of people because it's what you would have done in his place."

Morwenna stuck out her tongue in response. "At least I wouldn't have made such a hash of murdering my lover. Could he have possibly looked any more incriminating? Short of actually killing her on camera, he's done everything wrong. He's been seen out with her having a row, they leave together, he goes missing for several hours and then her body shows up in his business premises? It's the worst planned murder ever."

"Or the best set-up ever," Morgana said, thinking it over. "I mean, don't you think it's all too perfectly obvious? No other suspects at all. If someone planned this then it was done brilliantly, the police aren't really even looking for anyone else because the solution has been handed to them on a plate." She warmed to the idea. "Someone who knows Kendra's movements, who also knows Gregory's, pushes them together when he's in Bristol then somehow gets him out of the way and kills her, leaving her body in Portmage to incriminate him completely."

"There's a lot that could go wrong with a plan like that," Morwenna said sceptically. "And who knows both of them well enough to engineer it?"

"Someone must do, but no one here knows Kendra Allsopp, so it has to be someone from Bristol that Gregory keeps in touch with. I'll get into it tomorrow."

"Good luck with that." Morwenna reached and took a stack of cookies, then gave a pained sigh and put half of them back.

"You could help, you know, instead of sitting around on your fat arse doing nothing here all day." Morgana couldn't resist the dig.

"I came to see mum, but she's so busy running around after Ellie's off-spring, and you have your little shop of woo woo, what else am I supposed to do? I've walked around the village enough to be sick of it already, and it's too cold to lie on the beach. Plus everyone here just thinks I'm you and keeps trying to talk to me. I don't know how you put up with their inane comments about the weather all day long. Anyone interesting who grew up here moved away as soon as they could!"

"Gee, thanks." Morgana said, wondering how many of the villagers Morwenna had insulted. "Tristan is still here, you seemed pretty pleased to see him again."

"Yeah, he's still got it. It's like I can feel the charisma coming off him and you can just see he'd still be stunning naked. I'm not sure I like the suit though, it's like he's too grown up now. I preferred it when he was all out bad."

Morgana sipped her hot chocolate and regarded her sister with amusement. "Why do you always like them bad? Wouldn't you be much happier with a nice guy who treats you well?"

"I'd probably be bored. And, in answer to your question, I don't really know why I like them bad, it's just my type." Morwenna dunked a cookie into her chocolate and then lifted it into her mouth just before it fell apart. "It's your type too," she said through the mouthful of cookie.

"Huh? No, it isn't."

"Yes, it is, you just don't want to admit it. You and me, we like a little darkness with the sweetness. Why else did you go out with that arse-hat Ryan for so long?"

"Because I thought he was one of the good guys," Morgana protested.

Morwenna shook her head decisively. "No, you didn't. You wouldn't have been attracted to him if he was really as clean cut as he made himself out to be. You knew, you just didn't think he'd do it to you. We're witches, Mog, we have a little evil in us but we resist it. That makes us even better than intrinsically good people."

"How do you figure?" Morgana dipped her own cookie, which promptly broke in half and she watched with annoyance as the soggy end sank straight to the bottom of her cup.

Morwenna laughed at her. "Because you can't be brave if you don't feel fear. So you can't choose to be good if you don't feel temptation."

"I guess so," Morgana sighed and rose to tip her drink into the sink. It was ruined now. "Does that mean you're going to try to seduce Tristan into going out with you again, despite the fact he's become a bit more of a stand-up citizen?"

"Yes, I think I might do actually. I'd enjoy tempting him to be very naughty, just think how much more we could do now we're consenting adults."

"I can't imagine what you haven't done already. Whips and cuffs perhaps? What a shame you don't have a dungeon you can chain him up and torture him in." Morgana said, with slightly more edge than she'd intended.

"I'll torture him with my body instead," Morwenna licked her lips at the prospect. "And there's nothing wrong with a little bondage, Morgana, you can be such a prude sometimes. Poor Harry."

"Why do you say that? I can be fun!" She was nettled into replying.

"Yeah, but when are you going to be the real you? You've been buttoned up since Dad died. Suffocating the magic inside you, never really letting anyone close."

"You have no idea how hard it was dealing with my psychic abilities when everyone around me was in such pain. Being empathetic to their emotions while coping with my own made me physically sick." Morgana remembered only too clearly how she'd taken to her bedroom for weeks, trying to shut out the psychic battering of her family, and how she'd ended up literally curled into a corner shaking and sobbing.

"That's true, I thought you were going to eventually get locked up in a mental hospital."

They were both quiet for a minute remembering that traumatic time.

"Hence why I found a way to block it out. Only I can't get it back now." Morgana rubbed at her temples. "It would be really useful at times like this if I could read people a little better. I still get a lot from doing tarot cards, and a little bit if I'm touching someone, but imagine how easy it would be to identify a murderer if I could switch it on and off at will."

"True. But you can still open your third eye, right? View their psychic energy?"

"Yes, but it's too dangerous to do around anyone I don't completely trust as I can't see anything except the energy. I opened it a few months ago to view someone I suspected of murder and he almost killed me while I was incapacitated by the blindness and weakness that comes with opening it."

"So you don't know if Harry has nefarious designs on your virtue?" Morwenna teased.

"Not really. I can tell he's attracted, but not much more. I've been working on regaining my abilities, but it's slow going, I still need to be physically touching to get anything."

"Well, he must have a bit of bad in him or you wouldn't be attracted back. How physical do you need to get to be able to read someone? All the way? It would be hysterical if you were actually doing the deed and then sensed he was into pony play or something?" Morwenna grinned at her sister's outraged face.

"You have a twisted mind, you know that?" Morgana huffed.

"Which is why I'm a good subject to practice on." She held out her hands to Morgana. "Come on, try to read me, I'll project some thoughts and let's see what you can get?"

"Sure, okay." Morgana jumped at the chance. She'd been good at reading her twin when they'd been young, but she was getting nothing now. She reached across the coffee table and took hold of Morwenna's outstretched hands, closed her eyes and opened her senses.

The connection was fuzzy, flashes of images and feelings. She tried to concentrate harder. Morwenna's mood was different from how she'd thought. It wasn't nearly as light as her sister had pretended, instead she sensed deep introspection, and anger, and a strong desire to crush those that stood in her way.

Morgana pulled back slightly in shock. She'd known her sister was ambitious, but the force with which she intended to get what she wanted was new to Morgana. She let go of Morwenna's hands but Morwenna gripped her fingers tightly.

"Don't stop, I can see from your face it's working. Now get ready for a visual."

Morgana kept her eyes shut and waited, still only getting flickers of colour and unclear pictures that vanished too fast to see properly. Quite suddenly, it came into focus.

She was driving down a city street, lights flashing by as she drove recklessly fast. She was in an open top sports car, the wind in her hair, she felt like she'd take off and fly if she went any faster, and she pressed down even harder on the accelerator. She laughed with crazy exhilaration and realised the laugh was Morwenna's and not her own.

She ripped her hands free from Morwenna's and opened her eyes to stare at her sister. "I was you! I saw a scene through your eyes, in a car?"

Morwenna nodded. "I was projecting a memory."

"Were you high? That was dangerously fast."

Morgana felt sweaty just thinking about it.

"High on adrenaline, nothing else. The car was stolen. You asked me earlier if I had a criminal record, so I thought I'd show you."

"Bloody hell," Morgana said with feeling, wiping her brow.

Morwenna grinned. "It was a strong memory, and most importantly it worked! You saw what I was thinking."

Morgana gave a weak smile. "That's true. But you are my twin sister, we're supposed to be attuned."

"Then start working on doing it with other people. Next time you're snogging Harry, see if you can peek inside his kinky mind."

Morgana shook her head. "That doesn't seem fair."

"You need to use your power, Mog. You are a witch, deal with it or you're only half the person you're meant to be. And just think, if you'd read Ryan then you wouldn't have caught him with his pants down, you'd have known it was coming and left him a long time beforehand."

"I suppose so," she admitted.

"And while you're at it, can you read Tristan for me? I want to know if he's going to stir my cauldron or turn me down."

"Well, I suppose in the interest of research, I could always snog him too," she said, just managing to keep a totally straight face. She ducked as Morwenna picked up the whole box of cookies and hurled them at her head.

Chapter Twelve

Morgana was shocked at Gregory's appearance. He looked thinner and there were heavy dark circles around his eyes. She shot an accusing look at Tristan who held up his hands. "I wasn't in charge of his interviews, Morwenna. You need to take it up with the Inspector if you think he's been unfairly treated, but try to remember that we are dealing with murder. It doesn't get much more serious than this."

"Are you going to hover over us while we talk?" she said, still looking at him with disdain.

"No, but PC Dunn has to stay, okay? It's standard procedure."

Morgana looked back into the interview room and saw Poppy Dunn sitting in a corner looking bored. She nodded her acceptance and went in. Tristan watched suspiciously for a moment as she gave Gregory a hug, then closed the door when she took the seat on the opposite side of the table.

"How are you?" Morgana reached out and closed her hands around Gregory's cold fingers. She opened her senses as much as she could, but all she could pick up was fear. He was totally consumed by it.

"I'm okay." She saw a flicker of his aura as he told the simple lie. That was something, she supposed. Being able to pick out a lie was a good start. But she couldn't bring herself to ask outright if he'd done it. It might give her a definite answer if he lied to her, or it might just really hurt him that she could even ask such a thing.

"Tell me about Kendra Allsopp," she said, letting go of his hands before it got weird.

Gregory slumped, and she knew he'd probably said it all a hundred times already but she needed to hear it for herself.

"She was our secretary, years ago."

"Our?"

"My first company. I was at Bristol Uni with a guy called Simon Blake, we were both doing Business Studies. My dad ran a commercial property company, his dad was a baker. We were paired together for a pretend start-up and it went from there. We were only twenty-one, but we realised that between us we had the contacts to actually open a bakery. Bristol is a university city, and we identified a niche for meat pies. Small warm pies as a quick hearty lunch, big pies they could just shove in the oven at home. It was a cheap and tasty way to fill up which appealed to the student market. Our first bakery was in the heart of the student village, but it was so successful we quickly expanded into the suburbs too. We hired Kendra when Simon's mother retired. She'd been doing all our books until then."

"How long ago was this?"

"Um, let's see, I was about twenty-five I guess, so maybe nine years ago? It was the year before I met Ellie."

Morgana thought carefully about how to phrase her next question. "Did you and Kendra have any kind of relationship? Before you met Ellie, of course."

He shook his head. "Never, I promise. I knew she had a thing for me, but I wasn't interested in her that way." He put his head in his hands. "I had to be quite harsh with her, she seemed a bit obsessed at times. Which was why I didn't keep her on when Simon and I parted ways. She was one of the reasons our partnership soured actually."

Morgana chewed her lip. So far as she could sense, he was telling the truth. And she couldn't see any possible motive for murder. "What happened?"

"Simon liked Kendra, and she liked me. It was awkward. He and I were out having a few beers one night and I suggested letting her go, it got heated and he punched me."

Morgana leaned forward, finally seeing something she could work with. "So, he's got a temper? He could be violent?"

Greg shrugged miserably. "Not generally."

"But when it came to Kendra?"

"I don't know. We'd had a lot to drink that night..." Gregory tailed off. "We patched it up, but not long after that I went to Cornwall and met Ellie. It seemed like a logical time to go our separate ways. We divided the business without much animosity. He has no reason to want to see me in prison. Putting her body in my Portmage business just isn't him."

"But if he killed her in a rage and then didn't know what to do with her, using you to plant her on does make sense." Morgana felt excited by this lead, it definitely had potential. "Have you told the police all this?" Morgana looked over to Poppy, who was pretending to read a magazine but obviously listening to every word.

"Yes, of course I have."

"But Tristan, I mean, Detective Sergeant Treharne," said you weren't answering their questions."

"He wants me to admit to seeing her on the night she died," he said in a low voice. "And my lawyer says I shouldn't answer any questions."

"Oh, for goodness sake, Greg. They have video footage of you together." Morgana threw up her hands in frustration. "Just tell them everything."

He shook his head, remaining mute on the subject.

"Okay, fine. Tell me more about Simon Blake. Do you think he was in love with Kendra?"

"I haven't seen him for years, but I suppose he was pretty keen on her back then. He offered her a huge pay rise to stay with his side of the business when we went our separate ways. That was the last I saw of either of them. She's tried to contact me a few times, but I always said I was too busy to meet her."

"Until the night she was murdered," Morgana pointed out.

Gregory folded his arms defensively and said nothing.

She didn't get much more out of him after that, and after promising to look out for Ellie, she left.

"So, he wouldn't tell you anything either?" Tristan said, as she stopped at the door to his office.

"No. I'm sorry. Who is this lawyer that thinks he should stay silent? It's ridiculous."

Tristan nodded, "I agree, but I suspect that his version of events probably make him look even more guilty. He must have something to hide. My best guess is that if he didn't murder her then he was having a relationship with her, and he doesn't want his wife to know about that."

Morgana had to concede it sounded possible. He could be hiding the truth so that Ellie didn't discover that he'd ever cheated on her. After her own experience with a cheating boyfriend, she had to accept that you never truly knew.

"Can't a post-mortem tell you if she, you know, had sex or anything the night she died?"

"It can," he nodded, "and she didn't. But that doesn't mean they haven't before."

"No, it doesn't," she said, feeling depressed at how crappy people could be. "Have you followed up on Simon Blake?"

"Not personally. The Avon & Somerset force handled it. Kendra Allsopp worked for Simon Blake for the last eight years, but she handed in her notice when she came into her inheritance. Apparently, he hasn't seen her for three months. They couldn't find any contact between them since then, and no motive." Tristan looked apologetic.

"But Gregory seems to think Simon had feelings for Kendra? Isn't it possible that he was upset by her leaving?"

"Maybe, but I can't go stamping into their territory. I have to take their word for it."

"But I don't," she pointed out.

"Look, I know you want him to be innocent, but chances are he's not. I'm sorry. Do you really think you can learn anything they can't?"

Morgana got the feeling that Tristan was somehow deliberately goading her to go and check it out. Maybe he felt it hadn't been properly investigated? But he kept his face impassive and she couldn't tell. Darn her lack of powers!

"Maybe I can, maybe I can't. I'm going to Bristol anyway," she decided out loud.

Chapter Thirteen

"Would you like some company?" Harry asked as Morgana filled him in on her plans. She'd gone straight back to the shop and asked Morwenna to hold down the fort, only to find her sister totally uncooperative. So, she'd pulled out the big guns. Her mother.

"Put her on the phone," Delia instructed.

Morgana held the phone out to Morwenna, who looked extremely truculent as she took it.

"I don't want to spend the day stuck in a poxy shop," Morwenna whined. "She can close for the day, who would care?"

"That's not how things work here. In a small village every single day matters. You can't run a business that way." Morgana could hear her mother scolding Morwenna.

"Ellie's business is closed," Morwenna pointed out.

"And it's hurting her reputation. People look elsewhere and don't always come back. She'd be open if she could, and she's losing money. She can barely function right now. Her husband is in police custody for goodness sake. So stop being selfish and help your family, that's what we do, we pull together!" Delia was direct and stern, and Morgana watched with satisfaction as Morwenna gave in ungracefully.

"Yeah, yeah, okay. I'll play shop girl. But it's for Ellie, not for Morgana." She gave Morgana a furious look for landing her in trouble and hung up the phone.

"I'm going to get a sales assistant for the summer, this really is a one off," Morgana said, feeling mean now she'd won the round.

"Whatever, write me a list of instructions and I'll go and shower. Oh, and I'll need more clothes." Morwenna stomped away looking moody.

Morgana went down to the shop and was just finishing off the list when Harry walked in.

"Hi," she gave him a smile, happy to see him. "Is this a social call?"

He gave her a suspicious look and his eyes went to her wrist. Morgana looked down and saw that her bracelet was hidden by the sleeves of her dress. She didn't say a word, just waited with interest to see what he'd do.

He strode across the shop floor, stopped right in front of her, and cupped the back of her head with his hand pulling her forward for a kiss. His lips demanded a reaction and she gave it wholeheartedly. His other hand moved to her back and then slid down pulling her close against him. She managed to gain a brief image of herself, her hair fanned out across a pillow before he broke the kiss with a look of challenge in his eyes.

"Wow, you were pretty sure," she said, impressed and more than a little turned on by his visualisation. It was a mental victory that she'd been able to sense his thoughts.

"Actually, I wasn't, but I figured it didn't matter either way. I could get my face slapped and claim ignorance, or I could get to kiss both of you," his voice was teasing, and she tutted at him.

"Dangerous game to play with witches," she spoke without thinking.

His eyebrows went up. "Witches?"

She realised her mistake and went for turning it into a joke. "Absolutely. *Double, double, toil and trouble.* There's two of us, double trouble if you mess with the wrong one."

"I knew it was you," he confirmed.

"Hmm," she said, not quite sure if she believed him.

"I have nothing to do with the bakery closed and wondered if I might be able to take you for lunch?"

"That sounds great, but actually I've decided to drive up to Bristol today and question Gregory's old business partner. He employed the dead girl until recently," she explained.

"Would you like some company?" Harry asked. "I got up early and went surfing and then realised I didn't have much to do with the rest of my day."

"That would be fantastic, though you'll have to put up with being rattled around in my ancient Land Rover. It's good for country driving but terrible at high speed on the motorway."

"Then let's take my car? It's a smooth ride and you can just relax all the way there," he suggested.

"Sure? Great, in that case I'm ready when you are."

Once Morwenna had taken over the shop, Morgana and Harry strolled together to the bakery where he'd parked his car in the reserved space at the back.

Behind the row of parking spaces, there was just rough grass all the way to the edge of the cliffs that looked out over Portmage Beach.

"If it *was* Gregory, then why put her body in the bakery?" Morgana said, looking out towards the sea. "It would have been so much easier to just tip it over the edge and let the waves carry it away. Instead he'd have had to carry a dead weight inside, knowing for sure that it would be found the next morning, and then he drove away?" She shook her head. "It doesn't make sense."

"Perhaps it was guilt? Maybe he wasn't thinking straight after what he'd done, and subconsciously he wanted to be caught?" Harry suggested.

"Perhaps," Morgana agreed, unconvinced.

"It's so beautiful here, not a bad place to die." Harry shaded his eyes against the midday sun and looked towards Portmage Point, where the silhouette of the castle rose up against the backdrop of blue.

"Yes," she agreed. "Some people find this coastline unforgiving. It doesn't have the soft sands of the south coast, but it's far more dramatic."

"And rugged, let's not forget that, I'm told women like rugged." He slid and arm around her waist pulling her a little closer.

She gave a small laugh which turned into a shiver as the wind pulled at the long skirts of her dress, almost as if urging her to move. It always did that, tugging her toward the castle. She suspected that one day she was going to have to deal with the past that lingered in those ruins, but not today.

"Nice car," she commented, running her hands over the sleek silver bonnet. "Is it economical on petrol?" She thought of her own ancient Land Rover which guzzled gas.

He gave an apologetic lift of his shoulders. "I feel like I ought to give a technical answer to that. Does it make me less of a guy if I don't know a thing about cars?"

"You know a thing or two about pastry, that more

than makes up for it."

"In the Loire, everyone drives an old banger. They pootle about the countryside half-cut on local wine, and it doesn't matter if you occasionally drive into a ditch." He grinned at the memory.

"It must have been wonderful living in France all those years," she said, getting into the passenger side as he started the car. "The food, the wine, the cheese." She licked her lips, just thinking about all the wonderful cheeses of the various regions.

"That's what really matters in life, right? Though, I will miss this place, the sound of the sea in the night."

"Are you leaving?" She turned in her seat to look at him, upset by the thought.

"Oh, only for a few days, don't worry. I'm going back to France at the weekend, just catching up with some old friends. I did clear it with Ellie a while ago."

His aura flickered into sight, but it came and went so fast that she didn't get a good look. But she recognised a lie in the colour. She turned back to stare at the road ahead.

Why had he just lied, and what exactly had he lied about? That he'd cleared it with Ellie? No, that would be a stupid thing to lie over because Ellie would say something. It had to be his reason for going. He wasn't going to catch up with old friends? What else could he be doing? The answer came to her quickly. It was probably something to do with his ex-wife and he didn't want to say when they had only just started seeing each other romantically.

That was okay with her. If she had to see her ex-boyfriend for some reason, Harry was the last person she'd want to talk about it with. Instead, she focussed on asking him questions about French regions and the car ate up the miles as they discussed food.

"Where exactly are we going?" he asked as he came off the motorway and navigated through the traffic of Bristol city centre two hours later.

Morgana looked at the address she'd found on her phone. "He apparently has an office in Clifton, on Victoria Street."

"Okay," Harry changed lanes.

"You know where that is?" Morgana asked in surprise, as the tiny map in front of her indicated they were now heading in the right direction.

"I moved about a bit when I first came back to England. Before I found a new home in Portmage," he put a hand on her knee, indicating he was just as happy to have found her as to have found the village.

Morgana sensed his attraction at the contact between them and basked in it, leaving him to figure out where they were heading. She also picked up on some nervous tension in him, and she felt the same. It was exciting to be at the stage where you wanted to touch each other, to talk to each other, to discover everything, but it was happening pretty fast.

Being forced into close proximity by travelling in the confines of the car for a couple of hours had raised the level of intimacy, and she knew that if there hadn't been a murder and they'd both just been at work as usual, then things would have moved slower.

"This is Victoria Street," he said, pulling up in a parking bay.

She scanned the buildings then pointed to one a little

further down. "That's it, now we just have to hope he's there."

"Yes, and hope he doesn't throw us out when we ask him if he's committed murder!"

Chapter Fourteen

"Mr Blake will see you now." The young girl at the desk put down the telephone and indicated a door. "You can go on in."

"Thanks," Morgana and Harry went in and found a well-groomed man, sitting behind a desk. He stood up to shake their hands and then sat back down looking curious.

"Have a seat. I'm sorry, but I'm not sure if I'll be much help. You're working with the police on Kendra's murder? Such a shocking business! I don't think Gregory would ever do such a thing, it's unthinkable."

"We're not exactly working with the police," Morgana said, "I'm actually Gregory's…" She stopped suddenly as Harry kicked her in the ankle, and cottoned on to his warning. "That is, yes, we're expanding on their enquiries. I apologise if you have to go over the same things twice, we just wanted to be thorough."

"I'm not sure what more I can tell you," Simon Blake spread his hands. "As I said before, I haven't seen Kendra for months. She stayed with me until her inheritance came though, but the moment the money was in the bank, she left and hasn't been in contact since."

"It's interesting that she chose to stay with you and not with Gregory when you divided the business?" Morgana said innocently, fishing for information.

"I was in a position to offer her more money," Simon

replied, looking pleased with himself.

"But I understand that she had more of a personal connection with Gregory?" She pushed to try to get a bit extra out of him.

"She wanted more from their relationship, but I don't think it was reciprocated. It wasn't really any of my business. I assume they stayed in touch, but he and I didn't part on the best of terms, so I don't know for sure. After she found out about her inheritance, she did mention that she was thinking of visiting him."

"Really? In Cornwall?"

"Sure, a holiday I guess. I didn't pay a lot of attention. Kendra and I used to talk a lot, but you know how it is, time goes by and you start to take each other for granted. I thought something might happen between us once upon a time, but the years went by and she got older and my feelings fizzled out. She did say something about how a friend of hers was encouraging her to renew things with Greg, and I thought it was a good idea. They always got on well enough, and then Debbie was looking for a job at the time and I thought she'd be a good fit for this office. Young and enthusiastic, customers like that." Simon shared a knowing smile with them, but both Morgana and Harry looked blank.

"Debbie?" Morgana asked, confused by this new name.

"She showed you in, pretty girl don't you think?" he directed this at Harry.

Morgana looked at him with distaste. "So Kendra was past her prime, but Debbie was willing to step into her role as a bit of crumpet in your office?"

Simon paused and eyed Morgana suspiciously. "Is this

relevant to the investigation? Which department did you say you were from?"

"I didn't," Morgana said, meeting his eyes with a challenge.

Simon stood up and smoothed down his jacket. "I'm sorry, I'm a very busy man. I don't know much about Kendra's personal life. I would suggest you contact her friends instead of her employer. You know how women are, they chatter constantly don't they? She had a close friend she shared everything with, always prattling away on the phone during office hours. Or her boyfriend, if he's still around."

"What can you tell me about her boyfriend?" Morgana said, staying seated.

Simon blew out a breath of irritation. "I don't know who he was, but she only met him a couple of weeks before she left. I don't think it was serious. I overheard her gossiping during one of her ridiculously long phone conversations when she was supposed to be working. I got the impression that her best friend didn't approve of him. Maybe you should be wasting his time instead of mine?"

Morgana opened her mouth to ask more questions, but Simon pushed the intercom on his desk. "Debbie, we're done here."

Harry stood up. "One last question if you don't mind, do you know the name of either the boyfriend or Kendra's friend?"

"No." Simon's answer was firm, and Morgana gave in and also stood up.

"Thank you for your time," she said, with chilly politeness. She waited until they were out on the street before exploding, "What a creep! And he was wearing a toupee. I hope that poor office girl doesn't fall for his smarm."

Harry shook his head, silently laughing at her. "She was wearing an engagement ring on a chain around her neck. I suspect she knows her boss wouldn't be happy if he saw it on her finger. he's probably smarter than he realises."

"That was very observant of you," Morgana said, "I didn't notice it."

"It was tucked into her shirt, but it was visible when she leaned forward."

"Oh, I see, you just happened to look down her cleavage?" She elbowed him in the ribs.

"Male instinct," he said, pulling her close and hooking a finger into the neckline of her dress to make a show of checking out her own cleavage.

Morgana was about to kiss him when a brilliant red glow caught her eye in a nearby car. Startled, she turned her head to look. She knew the aura of anger when she saw it. The person in the car was staring at them, but the pulsing red glow around them stopped her from being able to see whoever it was. She took a step to get closer for a better look, but the car engine instantly roared into life and pulled away.

She'd seen that red-hot fury once before when facing a murderer.

Chapter Fifteen

"So, do you think the drive was worth it?" Harry asked as they got back onto the motorway. "Did get what you wanted?"

"Not really," Morgana said, closing her eyes and thinking over what she'd learned. "Much as I disliked Simon Blake, I don't think he's really a suspect. He was far more interested in his new secretary than his old one, so there goes his motive of being angry at losing her."

"Which means you're back to having no suspects except Gregory."

"Not quite. There's still the boyfriend, and no one's found him yet." She was glad to have that to cling on to at least.

"It didn't sound like much of a relationship if it was fairly new and she was considering ending it anyway?" Harry pointed out.

"Maybe. I wonder if the police have talked to her best friend, whoever she was? Tristan didn't mention it." Morgana tried to remember exactly what he'd said.

"Tristan?"

"Detective Sergeant Tristan Treharne. He went to my school." She found herself reluctant to tell Harry more than that, and silently wondered why. Because Tristan had been her first crush? Or because he'd been Morwenna's first boyfriend? Neither reason was very good. "Anyway, I should call him and let him know what we found out."

"Of course. But you might need to start accepting that things look pretty stacked against Gregory. I know that Ellie is having an awful time of it right now and doesn't have space to worry about the bakery, but if the worst should happen, then she'll still want her business to focus her energy on. Being closed as we get to the busy season is going to hurt her financially. Do you think it would help if I reopened on her behalf? I know the waitresses would want to help her as much as they can too."

"That is incredibly sweet of you, Harry," Morgana said, putting her hand over his as he changed gear.

"Hey, I'm an all-round good guy." His fingers briefly squeezed hers before returning to the wheel. "And having you think the best of me doesn't hurt my cause." He gave her a devilish grin.

"Maybe if Morwenna is sticking around for a bit longer then I could help out too, restocking the jam or something?"

"That would be great, actually. There was a load of fruit ready for jamming and it won't keep long if it doesn't get done. The jam was always something Ellie did herself, and far better than I ever could."

Morgana had her suspicions about what extra ingredients Ellie was throwing in to make it so good, namely the odd magical charm. Nothing like a bit of magic to give something the edge over everyone else's. Which was something she couldn't do, but she was sure she could manage a basic jam.

"How about we get into the bakery tomorrow?" Morgana suggested as they arrived back in Portmage. "I still have the keys, and we'll need a day won't we, to get on top of the prep before reopening?"

"Sounds good. Why don't you check with Ellie and then give me a call?" He stopped outside Merlin's Attic but didn't cut the engine.

"I, uh, don't actually have your number," she said, slightly embarrassed to be the one to ask first.

He fished around in the pocket of the car door and found an old receipt to write on and a pen. "No worries, here you go." He gave a grunt of annoyance as the pen refused to work, and she bit back a smile at how much it felt like two awkward teenagers both trying to play it cool. Finally, he managed to scribble it down, and she took it, tucking it into her wallet.

"Thanks for coming with me today," she said as the awkwardness rose even higher at saying goodbye. She wanted him to kiss her but making out in the car in a public place was not high on her list of romantic moments. She looked down the road, which still had plenty of people wandering up and down looking in shop windows, despite the fact it was now early evening.

"My pleasure, and we'll hopefully get to spend tomorrow together too. You can tell me what your pet policeman thought about your theory on Kendra's boyfriend."

"My pet policeman?" Her mouth quirked.

"The one with the very Cornish name, Trevellyan?"

"Treharne. Yes, I'll speak to him tonight if I can." She opened the door, disappointed at the lack of kissing, and completely forgot she was wearing a seat belt which instantly tightened, pinning her back.

Harry chuckled, and leaned across to release it. But he didn't move away, instead he trailed his hand slowly up the belt, drawing it back from her body, and she sucked in a breath as his fingertips brushed against her neck and stopped there.

"This isn't the time or the place," he said, not moving his hand away, "but I'm looking forward to tomorrow."

"Tomorrow," she nodded, slightly nervous at the look of promise of things to come in his eyes.

He let go and she scrambled out of the car in an unladylike manner. She let herself into Merlin's Attic and then leaned back against the door, resisting the urge to fan her face.

"That good in bed, is he?" Morwenna said, making her jump as she appeared at the doorway at the top of the stairs. "You have the look of a girl whose been well and truly pleasured."

"I'll have you know that we did no such thing, he didn't even kiss me goodbye." She tried for a sharp tone, but it came out somehow smug.

"Darling, if he can make you look like that just by being in his presence then I'd jump him the first chance you get!"

Morgana climbed the stairs, thinking that maybe, for once, Morwenna was absolutely right.

Chapter Sixteen

"These will keep for at least a week, and I've made plenty." Harry placed another batch of pies into the fridge and closed the door on them. "It's great that Morwenna didn't mind covering the shop again today."

"Oh, she minded," Morgana smirked. "But it's for Ellie, so unless she wanted to burn the only bridges she has left, she had to pitch in."

"I think it's nice that you all rally around, you're a close family. I envy that."

"Not all of us, there's one person who isn't here who should be." She took a moment to send thoughts of love and light in the general direction she thought that person to be.

"You mean your dad? Ellie told me about him, he drowned in a storm, didn't he?"

"*Presumed* drowned," she said, still refusing to let go of the dream that one day he'd return. "But no, I didn't mean him." She turned away, making it clear she didn't want to continue the discussion. "Morwenna was pretty mad about working in my shop again today, she kept banging on about how she was supposed to be 'resting'. I suspect she'll leave it a long while before her next trip home. But that's okay with me. I got given a lecture on my way here from the village matriarchs on my manners, and they didn't even give me a chance to explain that it wasn't actually me that had been the one to upset them."

"The village matriarchs?" He pushed his hair off his

forehead, looking sweaty but still sexy to Morgana's eyes.

"Three old ladies who spend their lives monitoring what everyone else is doing, then telling everyone else about it. It's part and parcel of village life."

"So, I'm learning." He looked amused. "What did she do to incur their wrath?"

"It seems that Morwenna decided she wanted some roses, but instead of simply buying some, she took a pair of scissors to the roses hanging over the wall at Mrs. Braintree's house and made off with them. Mrs. Braintree was understandably annoyed, but instead of apologetically prostrating herself, Morwenna informed Mrs. B that as the bits she cut weren't actually on her property the roses were fair game by law. It did not go down well."

"She's technically correct though." He gave her an expectant look as though waiting for her to argue the point.

"That's the least of my problems. She's sworn at one of my suppliers after they declined to help her get the boxes into the stock room, and now they won't come back; and she broke a crystal ball over a customer's head because he kept staring at her backside, and worst of all she overfed my cat on treats yesterday and now he follows her around instead of me!" This was the biggest sin of all so far as Morgana was concerned.

"She broke a crystal ball over his head. You could get sued for that!"

"Oh, she did it magically, so he thought he did it himself. She even had him pay for the damage." Morgana was still stewing on Morwenna bribing Lancelot to love her.

Harry gave her an odd look. "He thought he did it himself?"

Morgana stilled as she tried to think of a way to take back her words. After a moment of deliberation, she decided not to even try. If Harry was going to become a part of her life, then it would be easier if he knew the truth about her family.

"Morwenna uses energy to shove objects with just her mind. Low level telekinesis," she explained, watching him carefully to gauge his reaction.

He blinked at her, then laughed. "Right, does she use it to hide car keys too? Because mine are always a bugger to find."

She faked a reciprocal smile and gave up. It was always difficult to explain to anyone who didn't know her family and their history. At least here in Portmage, there were some people who believed. Her mind went to Tristan's mother, who'd accepted it as perfectly normal, but that only happened with people who'd grown up knowing all about it and saw no reason to doubt it.

Portmage was steeped in so much history that myths and magic were part of the scenery.

"Did you manage to talk to the police last night about what we discovered in Bristol?" Harry asked as he set out everything they needed to make the jam.

"I did. Tristan assured me he was still looking into the boyfriend angle. They don't have any information on a best friend though, they couldn't find anyone who seemed close to Kendra. Certainly no one has come forward full of grief. Apparently, there was a number that she called often, but it was to a pay-as-you-go mobile phone so not actually registered. It's not on, so they can't trace it. That seems suspicious don't you think?"

Harry shrugged. "Not really, people move around, move on. Maybe her friend doesn't even know."

"It's depressing that she's not even missed. She was totally estranged from her father and had no idea she was eventually due to inherit millions. Maybe she'd have lived a different life if she'd known." Morgana said, feeling introspective.

"Not been running after a married man, you mean?" Harry was unmoved by the sadness Morgana felt, but it was reassuring that he was so contemptuous of such a thing.

"We don't know that's what she was doing."

"No," Harry agreed, "in my experience it's usually the man doing the chasing." He looked moodily down at the fruit box he'd just retrieved from the fridge. "Fancy helping with cutting some rhubarb?"

Morgana nodded, glad for the change of topic. "Is that a good seller?"

"Not particularly," he smiled. "But it's in season, so it's fresh. Fresh fruit makes better jam."

"I always heard you were supposed to use old or damaged fruit?"

"That's a myth if ever I heard one. I suspect it started because it's nice to simply enjoy the fresh fruit and then you can pulp up whatever you don't fancy eating and cover the taste with sugar. But in reality, the quality of the jam is only as good as the quality of the fruit." He lifted some rhubarb to her nose and she sniffed it appreciatively.

"You're still going to need a lot of sugar though,

right? Rhubarb is bitter."

"Yes, that's true, but it gives off a lot of natural sweetness when you cook it. Anyway, the recipe I'm using has got a secret kick." He wiggled his eyebrows at her.

"Who do I have to sleep with to find out the secret?" Morgana teased.

"No favours required," he said, pecking a kiss on her forehead. "It's chilli. One red chilli, deseeded and finely chopped is all you need to put some energy into the finished product." He put her to work, cutting up the rhubarb and adding it to a large pot on the stove. She then juiced some lemons, prepared the chilli, and finally, poured in an equal amount of sugar to rhubarb.

"What's next?" she asked, stirring the bubbling pot that was now boiling on a high heat.

"The jam jars need to be re-sterilised before we can use them. Washed in hot soapy water and then oven dried for at least thirty minutes." He instructed.

"What a glamorous task," she pulled a face, but did as he'd said. "Now what?"

"Now I remove the froth and then we wait. This has to cool down before I can check if it's reached setting point."

"How do you know when it's right?" She asked with interest. Jam making was something Ellie normally did alone, so she could add her extra witchy charms to the mix in private.

"By touch. I stick my finger in it and see if it wrinkles." He laughed at her bemused expression. "I know, it doesn't sound very romantic does it?"

"Not so much. I prefer the way you normally talk

about food."

"Actually, today has been the most romantic day I've had in a long time. It's nice having you in the kitchen." He picked a bit of rhubarb out of her hair and they shared a smile. "In the meantime, let's get the labels written and stuck on to the jam jars?" He opened a drawer and pulled out a roll of white labels, each one featured a vibrant blue pixie with his hand dipping into a jam jar. Beneath the picture it said *Pixie's Place, Bakery and Tea Room.*

Morgana wrote the labels and Harry stuck them onto the jam jars taking care to make them all uniform.

"It would be good if pixies were real and could come in during the night to get everything ready each day, like in the story?" He said with a chuckle, when they were almost finished.

"That was elves, and they made shoes. Real pixies don't help at all, they're destructive little blighters, but at least they tend to stay away from populated areas." Morgana concentrated on her penmanship as she wrote out each label.

"Seriously? Pixies huh? I never know what you're going to come out with next," his voice was teasing, but she flushed.

"And now you know why most people think I'm weird."

He laughed, and pulled her close. Morgana was just melting against him when they were interrupted by an insistent knocking on the shop front door. Morgana looked through the serving hatch to the glass doors and saw a man standing there looking at them with an angry face.

Chapter Seventeen

"Saved by the banging," Harry commented, letting go of her.

"Probably just as well, this isn't the time or place either, and anyone walking by can see us in here." She gestured to the café windows that only had half curtains covering them.

"Not if we were on the floor they couldn't," Harry called after her cheerfully, as she moved through the café area to answer the summons from the angry man.

"I'm afraid the tea-room isn't open at the moment," she told him politely. He looked upset and she wasn't sure she would have risked opening the door if she'd been alone.

"I'm not here for tea and cakes. I want to know if this is the place where Kendra's body was found?"

Morgana regarded him suspiciously. "Are you a reporter?"

He looked momentarily taken aback. "No, I'm a carpenter." Then his expression changed as he understood the question. "I'm a friend of hers. I want to know what happened to her. No one will tell me anything, but someone has been arrested?" His eyes went past Morgana to Harry, who was now putting the jam into jars in the kitchen. "She was in there?"

"Yes, but I'm sorry, I can't let you in, there's nothing to see here now." She gave him a thoughtful look. "You say you were a friend of hers? But you haven't spoken to the police? How good a friend?"

"I was involved with her, on and off. Not that I've known for sure since she got that blasted inheritance. Yesterday was the first time I'd tried to contact her in a while. I didn't know she was already dead. One of her neighbours told me last night after I was yelling at Kendra's door for about an hour."

"Well, I'm extremely sorry for your loss, but I'm afraid we don't know anything much more than you do."

"Someone knows," he said, glaring at them both with hatred. His aura suddenly flared up and Morgana took a step back at the intensity of it. "I cared about her more than anyone else ever pretended to. So you can tell your boyfriend to keep his nose out of other people's lives!" He whirled on his heel and stormed away down the high street.

"What did he mean by that?" Harry said, looking outraged.

"That he's seen you before. Both of us, in fact. I didn't recognise him immediately, but he was the man in the car outside Simon Blake's office."

"Oh," Harry's face cleared. "Are you sure?"

"Yes, positive. Which means we *finally* have a new suspect." She didn't tell Harry that she recognised the man not by his appearance, but by his aura. But there was no mistaking it as far as she was concerned. That deep red heat of anger that had briefly pulsed around him, it wasn't normal. No one was usually that furious at two virtual strangers without a good reason, yet this man had been, which meant he was probably unbalanced and quite possibly dangerous.

She pulled out her phone. "I need to call Tristan so

he can stop him and question him. The Bristol police haven't exactly been bending over backwards to find anything to clear Gregory. But hopefully we can persuade the local police to do more."

"We? I think you mean *you*. Just how friendly are you with this cop?" He nudged her playfully, and she tutted at him as she placed the call.

It didn't take her long to get put through and then she told Tristan all about their visitor. "So, you see," she concluded, "he seemed really angry and he was both in Bristol and here. That merits some attention doesn't it?"

"Sure does. And if he's in Portmage then we can take him in for questioning. Can you still see him? Can you describe him?"

Morgana looked out the window and spotted the man further down the street. "He's about twenty-five, white skin but tanned, sandy coloured hair, jeans and a blue sports jacket."

"Okay, I'm radioing to PC's Dunn and Spencer. They're not far away from the village. Is there any chance you can keep track of him? Don't put yourself in any danger, though."

"No problem." She motioned to Harry that she'd be back in a minute and slipped out onto the High Street, keeping against the wall even though the man had his back to her.

She felt like a spy from a movie as she moved cautiously from doorway to doorway, the phone pressed to her ear, and her eyes fixed on Kendra's boyfriend.

He went right to the end of the street and then into the Pay and Display car park.

"He's reached his car," she whispered, peering around

the side of the Public Toilet block that was built by the entrance. "And his car's white! Just like the one Bradley saw in the middle of Saturday night."

"Bradley?" Tristan sounded confused.

Morgana gave a groan as she realised what she'd given away. "Your brother, he was coming home late on Saturday and he might have seen something, or nothing, I don't know."

"And I'm only hearing this now?" Tristan's voice went cold with annoyance. "Why were you talking to Bradley about it?"

"Um, it's kind of complicated. It would be better if I explained in person? Oh! Poppy and the other guy are here. I mean PC Dunn and Dunner." She waved frantically at the police car now blocking the exit of the car park and pointed to the white car.

Tristan huffed out a breath, clearly not appreciating her lame attempt at lightening his mood with humour. "You'd better come down to the station too. Now, if you don't mind."

"Yeah, okay," she sighed heavily as she made her way back to the bakery. Driving over to Westpoint wasn't exactly how she'd hoped to end her day with Harry.

"Do you want me to come for moral support?" Harry offered when Morgana told him about the broken window and how she'd basically blackmailed Bradley into keeping quiet about it.

"No, and I'm sorry to leave you to finish the jam on your own, but it shouldn't take all that long. But I'll call you later when I get back?"

"Absolutely, I'd be interested to hear what happens with the boyfriend too if you can discover anything. This could be the break in the case we've been looking for."

"We?" Morgana grinned at him. "Are we a crime fighting duo now?"

"Hey, we're doing better than the police in my opinion, and we both want to see Gregory cleared, don't we?"

Morgana showed her appreciation of the sentiment with a lingering kiss, then reluctantly turned to go. She'd have really enjoyed the day, puttering about making jam with Harry, if it hadn't been for the horrible murder hanging over them all. She just really hoped that Kendra's boyfriend would turn out to be guilty as sin and they could move on with their lives.

She also hoped Tristan wouldn't be angry with Ellie for withholding information. She was also pretty nervous to face Tristan herself. She didn't want to lose his respect. What if he didn't forgive her for approaching Bradley behind his back?

Morgana fished around in her handbag and found her keys. Her car keys and her shop keys were on the same ring, despite Ellie constantly telling her what a bad idea that was. It seemed they were all endlessly advising each other, but never smart enough to listen. *Maybe that's just how families were*, she thought, getting into the car.

The chain of thought made her remember Morwenna and she sent a quick text message.

Please give the cat his dinner, I might not be back for a couple of hours.

You're out of cat food, came the reply a few seconds later. *I gave him sardines instead.*

"Nightshade and nettles!" Morgana grumbled to herself. "He'll never touch the dry stuff if she spoils him like that. How hard could it be to walk to the grocer, it's right across the road? Lazy witch."

Her phone buzzed again with a second message: *Don't forget to put a cushion under your knees. Carpet burn is no fun.*

This time Morgana said some very rude words about her sister before chucking the phone into her handbag and tossing the bag onto the back seat.

She ate biscuits from the glove compartment as she drove, annoyed at the fact she wasn't eating something delicious cooked by Harry. He would have gone back to his place by the time she returned to Portmage, and she couldn't go chasing after him. That would look too keen.

Westpoint Police Station was quiet as she went inside, and she imagined it was probably *always* fairly quiet. Except maybe on Harbour Festival weekend, when hundreds of ships gathered up and down the coast and there were parties that got out of hand. No one had drowned though so far as she could remember, it was mostly people getting drunk and setting off fireworks. There had been that one boat that had driven right into the Belhaven Pier, and had caused a great deal of police activity, but it was hardly the crime of the century.

"In here, *now*," Tristan said, appearing at the door of his office before she'd even had time to reach the reception desk.

"Oh dear," she said, looking at the dark expression on his face. "I can see I'm in for a spanking."

He narrowed his eyes. "That's a very Morwenna-ish comment."

"I'm Morgana," she said, feeling her chin jut out just a fraction.

"I know, I just meant her influence is rubbing off on

you."

"Right, because I'm the boring one." Morgana wasn't sure why she was being so defensive; she just didn't really want Tristan angry at her.

"I thought you were the dependable one, until I spoke to my brother, that is," he said, crossing his arms.

"Dependable means the same thing as boring," Morgana replied as she went past him and took a seat.

"No, it doesn't. Listen, I know we've hardly seen each other in years, but the folks in Portmage speak pretty highly of you. It's true, they think you're a little odd with your tarot cards and love charms and so on, but they also say that you're kind and genuinely care, so forgive me if I totally fail to understand why you went to Bradley and suggested he kept quiet instead of coming to me!"

Morgana raised one eyebrow. "You've been checking up on me in the village?"

He blew out an exasperated breath and seated himself at his desk opposite her. "We check up on everyone, Morgana. It's part and parcel of a murder investigation. We look into the backgrounds of anyone who might be involved, we canvas local opinions, we talk to friends and co-workers and make a timeline of who was where and when. It's a long and detailed procedure. And it really doesn't help if people hide pertinent details."

"Yeah, okay. I know it was stupid. But Ellie thought that if she told you the window lock was already broken and not done on the night of the murder then it would incriminate Gregory further. She was scared, not intentionally being difficult."

"I get that, but Gregory isn't the only person with keys to the bakery is he?" Tristan pointed out.

"Well, no. But just because Bradley was the one who broke the window it doesn't mean the murderer didn't still get in that way. It's an easy window to climb though, and the back door only has a Yale lock so anyone could open it from the inside."

"Which we already know." He ran a frustrated hand through his hair. "It's not our first ever murder investigation."

"It's not mine, either," she said conversationally, despite the tension in the room.

Tristan gave a reluctant smile. "I know. Aiden told me. He said you even managed to get a full confession with a witness to verify it."

"To be fair, I didn't know I had a witness at the time. Did Inspector Lowen also tell you I was a suspect in Mr. Walken's murder?"

"You weren't, actually. I read the file. Just for research, of course." He leaned forward, looking interested despite clearly still being annoyed with her. "How did you get the confession?"

"Would you believe me if I said the answer is tied to my talents?" She gave him a speculative look.

"As a witch, you mean? You realise nobody in this station but me believes in any of that? I wouldn't either, if I hadn't grown up in Portmage and seen Morwenna in action once or twice. If you told anyone else, they'd think you were just playing the witch card to boost business."

"Which is part of how it works. People would be much more guarded if they thought I actually *could* read them, even a little bit. When they let their guard down, I can see more, or when their emotions are running high.

Some people are much easier than others."

She chewed her lip as an idea came to her. "The man you brought in today, Kendra's boyfriend, he's easy to read. I could see his fury inside him. I could help you to discover if he's guilty."

Tristan gave a firm shake of his head. "We don't allow civilians to interrogate suspects, or to scare teenagers into keeping quiet. What's this nonsense about your family cursing Brad? He says he couldn't go out at night and was seeing things?"

"Ellie lifted the curse," Morgana didn't even bother to hide the truth about the hex, she figured that she didn't really need to with Tristan.

"Hmm." He sounded pretty sceptical anyway. "I know you're all going through a terrible time right now, but I'd really appreciate you not dragging *my* family into it, okay?"

"I'm sorry, okay? It was stupid and next time I will make you my first call, but you know our gifts are real. Isn't there any way I can use mine to get another confession? Sometimes I can see when people are lying or even what they're thinking if we're touching."

Tristan went silent, mulling it over. "You can tell if someone is lying? That's a pretty valuable skill."

Morgana shrugged. "It's not always visible. But everyone's auras have different colours which mean different things. You get a flash of sickly yellow when people lie. Kendra's boyfriend was a dark red, which means anger. It also means he's one of the people whose auras are easier to see."

Tristan tapped his pen on the desk, still pondering on that. "Can you see mine?"

"Not really. You're guarded most of the time."

"That's something, I guess," he said, more to himself than to her.

"So, can I talk to him?" she pushed.

"Still no, but I tell you what, you can watch the interview and let me know if you see anything. PC Spencer is doing his photos and fingerprints right now, and we're just waiting for the Detective Inspector to get here before we begin taking a formal statement."

Morgana pulled a face. "I don't think DI Lowen is a fan of mine. He's not going to let me sit in."

"That's why we have the one-way glass. You can't be in the interview, but I'll sneak you into the observation room."

"Tristan Treharne! I thought you were all about the rules now?" she teased.

"I would be, but I don't think the Inspector is going to believe me if I tell him the truth."

"No. I'm grateful you do though."

"We've yet to see if it works. And I'm still not okay with you intimidating my brother, or Ellie's behaviour either. On the other hand, Bradley hasn't covered himself with glory. You're all of you on my black list right now." He got up and left the room, and she didn't need her gifts to know it was going to take him a while to forgive her.

Chapter Eighteen

The observation room was dimly lit, and Morgana was glad of that. She wasn't at all sure about basically spying on the three inside the interview room, and it felt uncomfortable.

She glanced at Tristan seated beside her. In the low light of the observation room, the ageing of his face was invisible and he looked so much like the teenage boy who'd left Portmage ten years earlier. For a brief second, she wished she was Morwenna, able to reach out and touch him. Her fingers itched to see if his thick chocolaty hair felt as rich as it looked.

He sensed her eyes and turned his head questioningly. She quickly looked back to the more brightly lit room in front of her.

"What do you see?" he asked.

Morgana tried to focus. All she saw at that moment was three regular people. PC Poppy Dunn had her back to them as she sat in a chair at a small table in the corner. She was writing something, but Morgana couldn't see what it was. Detective Inspector Aiden Lowen sat on one side of a larger table and Kendra's boyfriend on the other. But none of them had any visible aura. For a moment, she was worried it wouldn't work through glass and then she saw a ripple of pink pass over the suspect.

"I can see he's nervous, but that's probably to be expected. It must be unsettling being questioned in any situation," she observed.

"Can you see anything about the Inspector?" he said, curiously.

"Not a flicker. He's got strong shields up. Poppy is really tired though, there's a kind of pale brown coming into view at the edges of hers." Morgana leaned closer to the glass, reaching out to press her hands against it. "It's really tricky to accurately describe what I see. I'm totally out of practice too, it's harder than I thought it would be."

Tristan reached out and flicked a switch, causing a voice to come out through the speaker on her right, making her jump and lose concentration.

"Can you state your full name for the record please?" Detective Inspector Lowen said.

"Joseph Horden, everyone calls me Joe though."

"Mr. Horden, can you tell me where you were on the night of Saturday May 1st this year?" The Inspector got straight to the point.

"I was in Dubai. I didn't get back to England until Tuesday morning."

The Inspector's face didn't change expression at all, but Morgana saw Poppy blink and sit up, all tiredness forgotten. This was unexpected and could make the interview extremely short.

"I see, and you got your passport stamped to that effect I take it?"

"Of course I did, and I can produce about ten witnesses who were on the plane with me from the construction job we'd just completed."

Tristan looked at Morgana, who had just banged her head on the table in a gesture of frustration.

"It would be hard to fake that," he commented.

"He's telling the truth," she said, in a heavy voice. "He's totally wide open, and his aura is mostly blue."

"Which means what exactly?"

"That he's not hiding anything, he's completely innocent." She rolled her shoulders. "Damn, damn and blast!"

"Have you heard enough?" Tristan said, compassion in his voice for the fact that yet again there were no suspects but Gregory.

"Yes." She followed him out of the observation room. "I suppose he must have gone to see Kendra on Tuesday and discovered the truth. Which was why he was outside Simon Blake's office on Wednesday and came down here today. He was just trying to piece it together."

"That sounds feasible. Though he could have saved us all the time and effort if he'd just gone straight to the police in Bristol. But it's quite normal for people to want to avoid dealing with us."

Morgana drove back to Portmage with her spirits at rock bottom. It wasn't until she stopped off at Castle Groceries for cat food on her way home that she discovered her wallet was missing. She rummaged through her bag frantically. Everything else was there.

"It's alright, love, you can pay me later." Mrs. Pendle said from behind the register. "It's not like I don't know you." She pushed the cat food toward Morgana.

"Thank you, Mrs. P, I promise I'll come in with cash tomorrow if I can't find it," she said, feeling like things could hardly get worse.

She wondered if she might have left her wallet at the bakery and after parking her car at the shop, she walked up the High Street to check. She was surprised and delighted to discover that Harry was still there.

"Morgana!" He greeted her with a smile that made everything seem a little bit less bleak. "I'm actually almost done, but I wanted to leave it perfect for Ellie. You look like you're badly in need of a cup of tea."

She nodded and left him boiling the kettle behind the serving counter while she did a quick search of the kitchen to see if she'd dropped her wallet anywhere.

"Did you lose something? You seem very low. What happened today?" Harry handed her a very welcome cup of tea and she leaned against the kitchen counter to drink it.

Morgana filled him in on Joe Horden and the fact that he'd been out of the country at the time of the murder.

"It seems as though everyone involved has no motive or they're in another country." She complained, blowing noisily on the tea to rid herself of her pent-up feelings of frustration.

"Except Gregory," Harry said, in a quiet voice.

"Yes," she agreed, miserably.

She was just feeling as though things couldn't get any worse when her phone rang again.

"Bloody hell," she fished out her phone and went into the front area to take the call where the reception was better.

"Morgana? It's Tristan. I'm afraid I have more bad news. I know that Gregory's barrister was hopeful of making a case based on the fact that we didn't have any physical evidence and it was all circumstantial, but we've found some. I'm sorry, but I thought you'd want to know."

"Something that definitely ties him to the body?" Morgana sat down on one of the chairs in the café area, feeling like the ability to stand had been taken away from her.

"No, but something that proves he went from Bristol to Cornwall that night and back again. A petrol station receipt. He filled up in Okehampton at 2am, and it's been calculated from what remains in his tank that the amount of petrol he used is exactly the amount he'd need to drive on to Portmage and then back to Bristol."

"Okehampton is less than forty miles from here," she said quietly, putting her head in her hands at such evidence.

So, it was conclusive. Gregory did drive to Portmage in the middle of the night for no good reason that she could see, except to maybe hide a dead body.

"Wait. Have you taken into account the fact that he then drove back here to identify the body?" she asked, still struggling to accept it.

He sighed. "Yes, of course we have. This is our job, Morgana. I appreciate the insights you've been able to provide, but it comes down to hard evidence in the end."

She put the phone down feeling both depressed and dismissed. It was awful being unable to do anything more, but she couldn't see where to go from here. Every other avenue was a dead end.

"What's wrong?" Harry put a hand on her arm, startling her.

She told him what Tristan had said.

"How could he be so stupid as to keep the receipt?" Harry looked stunned.

"You seem as surprised as I am that they've found

some conclusive evidence. I got the impression you'd decided he was probably guilty?"

"I didn't want to believe it. I'm so sorry. He must have used cash to pay for the petrol otherwise it would have shown up already on his credit card statement and they're bound to have pulled those," Harry mulled it over.

"I suppose so. In the meantime, I should get home. It's already six o'clock and there's not a lot more we can do to get the bakery ready for reopening. Just fresh bread to bake, right?"

"Yes, but don't forget that I can't help with any of that until the middle of next week. I've booked some time away for a few days, remember?"

"Oh no, I'd forgotten," she felt ridiculously in need of having him around. "When are you leaving?"

"It was going to be Saturday, but something has come up and I think it will have to be tomorrow. I'm sorry."

"Then can I see you later tonight or will you be busy?"

He looked hesitant. "I'll only be gone a few days, but yes, I do need to spend the evening packing. We'll make up for it after I get back, okay?"

"Okay."

"I'll just put the jam away, it's all done for now, and I'll get your coat and your bag from the kitchen. You take a load off."

"Thanks, you're an angel." She rubbed at her temples, wondering if she'd missed anything. She thought about the fact that Kendra's boyfriend had exhibited such anger towards them and wondered why. It had flared up when he'd looked into the kitchen. Was it because that's where her body had been? Or because he'd seen them in Bristol the day before and assumed they were involved or knew something he didn't?

"Great, Greg's going to prison, Harry is going away, Tristan is annoyed with me, and I have to go home to a cat-poaching witch!"

Five minutes later, Harry had finished his quick tidy and had locked up the café. They left through the back door to where he'd parked his car.

"You'll be just fine without me," Harry said, seeing the expression on her face. "I'll call you."

"My phone number is on the shop's website," she said, remembering that he'd given her his number, but she'd never given him hers.

He planted a brief hard kiss on her lips. "I'll be back before you know it."

She waved him off and noticed that the setting sun made the silver of his car seem to glow red as it reflected back the evening light. She was reminded of the red sea she'd witnessed on the dawn of Beltane.

"Bad times ahead," she murmured, staring after the car as something nagged at her. Something to do with silver… what was it?

Chapter Nineteen

"Girl, you look like you need a glass of wine!" Morwenna commented, turning off the TV as Morgana came in the door.

"Or whisky," she said, not even trying to hide her misery.

"What's up?" Morwenna asked, jumping up and fetching out two glasses and selecting a bottle of red from Morgana's drinks cabinet.

Morgana told her all of it. About Tristan telling her off, about Gregory being arrested and about Harry going away for a few days.

"He said I'd be just fine without him," she finished, "but I don't feel like I will, isn't that pathetic?"

"Yes," Morwenna agreed so soundly that Morgana looked up in hurt surprise. Morwenna shrugged at her sister's expression. "It's *completely* pathetic and not you at all. Since when did you need a man to feel like you could cope? You're a strong woman with your own business, magic powers, and perky boobs to boot. I know there's a lot of crap happening right now, but you're the capable one, you always have been."

Morgana sat straighter. "Thanks, Morwenna, that's about the nicest thing you've ever said to me."

"You still have a fatter arse than me though," Morwenna's smile turned wicked as she immediately countered her niceness by returning to form.

Morgana refilled her own glass and took another big

gulp. "You're right that I'm fine on my own, it's Ellie I'm really worried about, this will devastate her."

"Because her husband turned out not only to be a cheating scumbag but also a murderer? I think she'll get over him pretty quickly when she learns all the sordid details." Morwenna's lips thinned into a hard line of disapproval as she thought about Gregory.

"I don't know why he did what he did that night, but I still don't think he's a murderer, he's just not the type," Morgana said, shaking her head. "My powers are still not at full capacity, but I know people, Mew, and he's a good person."

"You still get it wrong sometimes," Morwenna said, not softening at all.

"Yeah, I do," Morgana admitted, all her conviction ebbing away.

"Look, it's going to be a miserable few days, especially for Ellie, and I'm not going to be around for much longer either," Morwenna regarded Morgana with a calculating eye. "But you are still going too far with your empathic thing. You don't have to take on everyone else's problems all the time. Tell you what, it's still early. What do you say to throwing on a bit of glitter and hitting the wine bar?"

"No, I'm too tired," Morgana argued, "And the wine bar is ridiculously overpriced, it's just for the London lot."

"*I'm* the London lot now, come on, up off your couch potato bum, my treat." She reached out and pulled Morgana to her feet.

"Your treat?" Morgana said, disbelievingly. "That has to be a first. But you don't get to pass the bill, because

I've misplaced my wallet. So you'd better mean it."

"I do. Let's show them all that we are still the hottest witches to come out of Portmage. I have a basque that gives a whole new meaning to breathless and you're going to leave them panting when you wear it."

"I'm going to leave them confused, they'll just think I'm you," Morgana grumbled as her sister manoeuvred her into her bedroom, but she didn't resist very hard.

Two hours later they stumbled out of the wine bar, both feeling very giggly.

"You were right, I needed that," Morgana conceded in a slurred voice as they wound their way precariously back to the High Street from the side alley where the bar was located.

They had just reached the main road when the sound of running feet made them both turn. A dark figure, with a hood pulled down low over his face, cannoned into them, sending both girls reeling.

"Hey!" Morgana yelled, as the figure grabbed her handbag. "Stop, my favourite lipstick is in there."

"Actually, your lipstick is in my pocket, I stole it when you went to the loo," Morwenna confessed, finding her feet first. "But it's still not okay. Watch this."

She stretched out her hands towards the retreating figure still running away from them, and made a sweeping motion. A metal dustbin rattled in a shop doorway and then the lid flew free like a Frisbee and spun through the air, hitting their assailant hard in his left arm and knocking him sideways. He dropped the bag, then spat out a curse and kept running.

"I don't think I've ever been mugged in Portmage before," Morgana said, as she reached her bag and bent to pick it up. The world spun slightly, and she toppled over. "Drat, I've turned into a total lightweight just when I need my wits. It's your fault for putting me in these stupid heels."

"Don't be silly, didn't you see how many men were looking at your ankles? The heels and leggings work considerably better than those long dresses you usually wear." Morwenna helped her to her feet.

"My ankles? Sure, why not. It's not as though we're in the Victorian era! Honestly, why would you even think I'd care about having a *nice turn of ankle*? Anyway, I have a boyfriend now."

"He's a man, and men are untrustworthy."

Morgana snorted in an unladylike manner. "Broad statement much?"

"Fine, name me a worthy one," Morwenna said, taking the keys out of Morgana's hand as she tried and failed to unlock the back door to let them into the flat.

"Dad."

"That's not fair. You can't play the dad card in this situation. He lived and died like a hero, no one is going to ever match up to him. That's why we're drawn to the anti-hero instead."

Morgana gave a drunken hiccup. "I need water, an entire pint of water, and toast with marmite."

"Now you're talking. The perfect way to avoid a hangover, I can't believe you got so drunk so quickly."

"Bad day," Morgana said, collapsing on the couch. "Bad, bad day."

"And you have to get up early to open your little shop." Morwenna gave an evil grin.

Morgana glowered at her. "If you were a great sister

then you'd offer to do it for me and let me sleep in."

"But we both know I'm not," Morwenna said over her shoulder, as she went into her bedroom and shut the door.

Morgana groaned and forced herself up to get some water and make toast.

She was going to pay dearly for this in the morning, and things were probably going feel ten times worse!

She was up and showered early, feeling reasonably well rested. "Just goes to show how old we're getting," she told Lancelot, as she gave him his breakfast. "Morwenna and I actually thought we'd had a big night out, turns out we were both fast asleep in bed by ten o'clock last night. Last of the big drinkers!" She chuckled to herself at how they'd genuinely been convinced they were still party girls, but at twenty-six they just didn't have the stamina that they'd had a few years earlier.

She remembered their eighteenth birthday, which was when they'd first legally been allowed to drink, and how they'd had a BBQ on the beach with a huge bonfire and still been dancing when dawn came.

It was the last time they'd all really been together. Delia and Ellie had made all the food, she and Morwenna had been surrounded by all their childhood friends, and her brother… Once again she sent love and light in his direction, wondering when the magic of Portmage would make him return. Probably not until he fell in love. That was also the year she and Morwenna had left home and gone off to different Universities. It had been a special summer, she thought, as she grabbed her broom to start sweeping. The future had held promise. Right now there seemed very little of that. Except maybe Harry?

She performed the ritual morning cleanse of the shop and cleared some space for a delivery she was expecting that day, then went out the front entrance and set off for the bank. The bank opened at nine and her own shop didn't open until ten, so she had plenty of time to get there and withdraw some money. She'd searched briefly for her wallet, but decided that it would be safest to cancel her cards just in case, which she could also do at the bank.

She stopped by the steps down to Portmage beach and took a moment, closing her eyes and breathing in the sea air.

The bark of a dog made her look down and she saw a West Highland Terrier sniffing at her boots. She gave a sigh and then forced a smile on her face as she turned.

"Good morning, Mrs. Goodbody."

"Miss Emrys," the older woman said in a cold voice. "I wanted to have a word with you. Cynthia Braintree told me that she'd seen you yesterday afternoon swimming in the sea topless! It's not a good example to set, dear. There are impressionable youths on the beach and watching a woman cavorting about in just her knickers is quite beyond what we consider acceptable here in Portmage."

"But I wasn't even in Portmage yesterday afternoon," Morgana said, outraged by the accusation. Then she closed her eyes as realisation hit her. "Morwenna!"

The other woman looked taken aback for a moment and then gave a slow nod. "Oh, I see. *She's* back, is she? Well, that explains a great deal."

"I'm sure she didn't mean any harm. She likes to swim with the seals you see. They know her…" She trailed off, not at all sure she was doing a good job of explaining her sister's actions. It was quite true that Morwenna had no need to be half *naked* when she did it. "She's not staying much longer, but if you think you see me acting strangely during the next couple of days, well…"

"I quite understand." Mrs. Goodbody squared her shoulders, "and I apologise for misjudging you, Morgana. A lady of morals will always rise above her birth. Give my regards to your *other* sister. I couldn't help noticing the tea-room has been closed all week, is she poorly?"

"No, she's just taking some time off," Morgana said, attempting to keep her smile in place, but actually quite amazed the village gossips were still unaware of Gregory's detainment and subsequent arrest. "Please excuse me, I must get to the bank."

She walked on extremely annoyed with Morwenna, who had clearly closed the shop and gone for a swim instead of helping out, but equally annoyed with Mrs. Goodbody for her comments.

"*A lady of morals will always rise above her birth*? What the hell's that supposed to imply?" She groused.

"Talking to yourself is the first sign of madness," Harry commented, his car pulling up beside her as she reached the bank.

"Harry," A genuine smile lit her face. "I thought you might have left already."

"No, I got delayed. I have some time and thought you might invite me back for coffee?"

"I'd love to, but actually I have to go to the bank and then it's opening time. I have a big delivery coming today and won't have time to sit and chat," she said, disappointed.

"How about tonight then? I'd invite you over to my place but it's a bit of a disorganised mess right now."

"No problem, come to mine. I'll make sure Morwenna's not there."

Her blew her a kiss and she smiled at the retreating car. It suddenly occurred to her that she hadn't asked Tristan if he'd questioned his brother about exactly what he'd seen the night of the murder. What had Bradley said? A white car without any lights? An insight nudged at her brain, but she couldn't quite pin it down.

She went to the bank and then stopped in at Castle Groceries to pay Mrs. Pendle the money she owed her and to pick up something for dinner with Harry.

"That's such a shame about you not finding your coin-purse, love," Mrs. Pendle said sympathetically, as Morgana bagged a few items. "Was there anything important inside?"

Morgana mentally went over the contents of her wallet and shook her head. "My bank cards, but not much actual money. A family photo I don't want to lose, and…" She trailed off, thinking of the little piece of paper she'd recently pushed inside. "I'm sorry, I've got to go." She grabbed her milk and rushed back outside where she pulled out her phone yet again, and found the number of Westpoint Police Station.

"Tristan, it's me. I'm sorry to bother you when you're annoyed with me, but I need to ask you an important question. Do you remember telling me that Kendra

Allsopp's only surviving relative lived abroad? What country was she in?"

Chapter Twenty

Morgana got out of the shower only to find Morwenna in her bedroom going through her jewellery box.

"Eh hem!" she said, trying to make her sister jump, but Morwenna just lifted some earrings and held them up for inspection. "Would these work with my outfit?"

"I take it that means Tristan called? You look ridiculously overdressed by the way; this is Portmage not London."

"He sure did. It's not a *date* apparently, but I'll take what I can get. He's going to wonder why he ever left Portmage while I was still here to cream his corncob."

"How poetic. And, you have an extremely selective memory, he left because you ended it, remember?"

"A lot of water has passed under the bridge since then. I just don't know if we're any better suited now than we were then." Morwenna chewed on her lip, giving Morgana the first glimpse of genuine insecurity that she'd seen in her sister for years.

"Because he's changed, become an upstanding good guy?"

"No," Morwenna pouted, "it's because he was *always* an upstanding good guy hidden underneath."

"Well, if anyone can convince him *off* the straight and narrow, then it's probably you. Just make yourselves scarce before Harry comes. I can't have you ruining my chances this evening."

As Morgana applied her make-up, she thought about what Morwenna had once said about the fact that she, too, was drawn to bad boys. But Morwenna was wrong, that wasn't what she wanted at all.

"Meow?" Lancelot butted her arm, causing a streak of eyeliner to draw across her cheek.

"Yep, you're the only bad boy allowed in my life," she said, stroking a hand down his long black back. Her head snapped up as the doorbell went on the back entrance to the shop, and she quickly repaired her face before going down to answer it.

"Nice place," Harry commented, as she led him into the kitchen where she'd laid out some olives, crisps and a dip. He handed her a bottle of wine and she went to the kitchen to open it.

Harry followed and took two glasses down from the shelf for her.

"I thought you didn't drink?" she said remembering their first date when he'd only order cola for himself.

"I do drink. I mean, I'm not an alcoholic or anything, I *can* drink, I just prefer not to sometimes." He gave a rueful smile. "And I never drink and drive."

"But you didn't have your car last Saturday night when we went to the pub, did you?"

Harry put his arms around her from behind and placed a kiss on her neck making her shiver. "I needed a clear head, so I didn't say anything stupid and put you off."

"Is that so?" She leaned into him and opened her senses as wide as she could. She remembered her recent experiment with Morwenna and the level of concentration she'd needed to get a clear picture from her.

This was exactly the same, the connection seemed fuzzy, like a television station that wasn't tuned in. His mood was extremely difficult to read. Excited, maybe? But a dark excitement. Maybe it was lust and Morwenna had been right that he wasn't as vanilla as he seemed. It was still unclear, but she reminded herself that she'd got a visual from him once before. She'd seen herself with her hair spread out across a pillow, he'd been imagining her that way when they kissed, and she'd been able to view his thoughts. If she'd been able to do it then, surely she could do it now? But did she really want to?

She had to, she had to be sure!

She turned in his arms and increased the connection by kissing him, their bodies pressed firmly against each other as she probed deeper into his mind with her inadequate powers.

Flickers of colours, images that flashed and were gone too fast to focus on. She had no choice but to deepen the kiss. Then she had it. Once again, it was a vision of herself. But this time she was tied up.

Tied up and begging, tears running down her face.

She released him with a gasp of horror. That vision hadn't been his imagining some dominance game, it had been malicious. Unwholesome desire, not to possess her but to hurt her.

"Morgana?" Harry was looking at her with concern in his eyes, and she swallowed several times to find her voice.

"You needed a clear head on Saturday, but not to talk to me, it was so that you could drive that night."

"What are you talking about?" He threaded his fingers

into her hair in an affectionate gesture, and she forced herself not to back away.

"I'm talking about the receipt, the one you wrote your phone number on? It was evidence that you'd driven to Bristol that night. When I told you about the petrol receipt the police found that belonged to Greg, you acted like you were shocked that he'd been so stupid as to have kept it. But you weren't thinking of Greg, you were thinking of yourself. That was when you realised that you'd stupidly handed me a piece of evidence. Evidence that showed you were there too."

"So, you *did* see it? I wondered if you had." His hand clenched in her hair, gripping it so tightly that she yelped involuntarily.

He reached out and grabbed the corkscrew from the counter, bringing the sharp end of the twist up under her chin, then he dragged her by her hair over to the kitchen table and forced her down into a chair.

Morgana kept her eyes locked on his, watching, trying to see his aura, but he was calmer than she'd expected. Cold, emotionless. When she sat down he released her, but she didn't move, simply waited to see what he'd do next.

"When did you realise?" he asked.

"It first crossed my mind when I saw you drive off this morning. Your car's silver, it reflects moonlight, it would appear white."

Harry looked momentarily confused, but then he ripped the phone off the wall and stepped behind her, coiling the flex cord in his hands.

"I didn't want to have to do this," he said, as he pulled her wrists behind her and began to bind them with the phone flex.

"Don't you? I rather have the impression that you do." She gave him a look of disdain.

Harry pulled the cord tight with angry jerks until it dug into her skin. Then he came round the table and sat down in the chair opposite her.

"Where is it Morgana? Give it to me or I will kill you then find it myself." The look of determination in his eyes left her in no doubt that he meant it.

"It was you, last night, wasn't it? You tried to steal my bag?" she said, deliberately not answering his question. She didn't doubt for a second that he intended to kill her anyway.

"I couldn't leave without that receipt!" He banged his hand down on the table. "Or all that planning would be completely wasted!"

"What will you do if you can't find it?" She played for time.

"I'll be gone before anyone else discovers it. Unfortunately, you'll be gone too, so you can't tell anyone and stop me. You said it yourself, why would someone put a body in a bakery when they could simply tip it over the cliff and let the waves carry it away? That was it, wasn't it?" He waited for her response and she could only assume that he expected her to start crying and begging at this point. Well, she wasn't going to give him the satisfaction of playing it out as he'd imagined. She'd seen what he wanted, and there was no way she'd cry or beg. But she'd seen other things too and it confused her.

"Why did you start a relationship with me?" She asked curiously. "Wouldn't it have been much safer just to keep your head down?"

"In a village like this one? Credit me with a little intelligence! People here are wary of newcomers. I didn't want to seem like a suspicious character, and what better way to be accepted than to start seeing the pretty younger sister of my boss? I was going to keep it casual, but then you began trying to clear Gregory's name and it seemed smarter to stick close and see what you uncovered."

"But what about your wife? How would she feel about that? You *are* still married, aren't you?"

"Obviously, and it was difficult, but she would have understood. The money will make it all worth it."

"She'd have understood you kissing me the way you just did?" Morgana felt her own anger spiking inside her at being used that way.

He gave a humourless chuckle. "I can't pretend I wasn't tempted sometimes, Morgana. You are quite alluring. But I did it for love."

"Is that how you got to Kendra, too?"

"No," he shook his head. "Haven't you worked out that I was the missing friend? I spent weeks becoming her confidante, learning everything about her life so that I could plan the perfect murder."

"Of course," Morgana murmured, as more bits dropped into place. Simon Blake's comment about Kendra's friend.

"Maybe you should be wasting his time instead of mine."

She hadn't picked up on it, or had assumed it was a slip of the tongue. *His* time, Simon Blake had known Kendra's best friend had been a man and not a woman as everyone else had assumed, but annoyingly he hadn't made it very clear.

"She was a silly twit, no brains at all," Harry continued, conversationally. "Do you know that she actually believed Gregory would take one look at her new clothes and new hair and decide to leave his wife for her? I never thought she had a chance in hell, but I did think he might take her to bed. That would have made things so much easier."

"It was clever of you, putting in all that research," she said, trying to appear impressed. "It must have taken a lot of time."

He gave her a look of satisfaction. "It did. But we were talking millions. Kendra had lost touch with her father, but Marianne hadn't. If Kendra wasn't around then Marianne would inherit the lot. *We* would inherit. Marianne and I need the money, she's unhappy and this will make her happy. We knew Kendra's father was dying months before it happened. The important thing then was to put as much distance as possible between the two of us, so that I'd never be suspected. Marianne and I deliberately separated and I came to England before he even died. But six months apart is nothing when you consider what we'd gain."

Harry's eyes took on a manic gleam. "It just required patience, and discovering the right scapegoat. Once Kendra had told me everything I needed, I came to Portmage and waited for the perfect opportunity. Your sister was so pleased when I came looking for a job." He grinned and she resisted the urge to give him a slow clap. Not that she could anyway, with her hands still tightly bound.

He leaned across the table, looking menacing. "Which

brings me back to my question. Where is the receipt?"

"Kendra's boyfriend recognised you. He'll work it out soon," she told him, avoiding a direct answer.

She remembered now. *Tell your boyfriend to keep his nose out of other people's lives!* That's what Joe Horden had said. She'd thought at the time it was a strange thing to say. Why not tell *her* to mind her own business too? But it made sense now.

"Yes, it would have been nice to have tied off that loose end. I tried to ruin their relationship, but he was persistent, and having him see me here wasn't ideal." Harry clenched his fist again. "But it didn't matter, I just had to bring forward my plan to leave England."

"Back to your wife in France? You must know you'll need to go a lot further than that to escape justice."

"Obviously, but I thought we had some time. Marianne has to actually collect the inheritance before we disappear forever. Gregory is the one who'll go to prison, not me. Unless you've ruined everything? It was perfect, he practically walked right into it. But then you just had to go and stick your nose in, didn't you? It would have been better if you'd just let me leave. It wasn't my intention to kill you."

"Do you *have* to murder me too? Morwenna's spending the night with a man, you could be long gone before anyone finds me tied up in here?" Morgana suggested.

"Is this the point when you promise not to tell anyone? That's too cliché for you, surely?" he raised an eyebrow mockingly and rose to his feet.

"You know what cliché I hate?" Morgana said. "It's the one where the girl in the movie runs headlong into a dangerous situation all alone and forgets to tell anyone where she's going. It's not very realistic is it?" A smile flickered over her face as she remembered the last time she'd confronted a murderer. She'd stupidly been all alone that time. Then again, she hadn't believed he would hurt her. This time she didn't doubt it at all. Harry was definitely intending to kill her and dump her body into the sea.

He stilled, looked at her expression with wary suspicion. "You don't seem very scared."

"That's because I'm a witch, Harry," she said, in a strong West Country accent. "Hexus!" She shouted the last word, and he stared at her, waiting for something to happen.

"Was that supposed to be magic?" he sneered.

"No," a voice said from behind him. "But this is." Morwenna flung out her hands and all the saucepans on the shelves cascaded down, forcing Harry to cover his head with his hands as they crashed and bounced off him.

Tristan raced out of the spare bedroom, around Morwenna, and threw himself on top of Harry, wrestling him down into the floor and planting a knee in his back as he pulled Harry's arms behind him and snapped on handcuffs.

"Did you get enough?" Morgana said, her body slumping as the adrenalin drained out of her.

"We got it all," Tristan confirmed.

"Then would one of you please be so good as to untie me? My wrists are killing me."

"Not literally they aren't," Morwenna said, taking her time as she stopped to kick Harry extremely hard in the left arm, right where she'd struck him with the dustbin lid.

Chapter Twenty-One

It took two hours for the paperwork to be processed, and then Gregory was a free man. Ellie went to collect him in a taxi while Delia watched the children, who were fast asleep as the hour was now late. Morgana and Morwenna sat on the couch in their mother's living room and ate left-over fish-fingers.

"You doing okay?" Morwenna asked in a low voice, as their mother went to get them refills of the sweet sherry that she enjoyed, and the others barely tolerated. But Morgana felt she was in need of something to take the edge off.

"Yeah, I'm fine."

"You look exhausted."

"That too. It's still a real struggle to use my powers, and not always a pleasant experience when I do."

"I don't know, all the lip smacking sounded very pleasant. And you have to admit he was still smoking hot even if he was a psycho." Morwenna nudged her, but Morgana ignored it.

"You didn't see what I saw," Morgana's voice betrayed her pain.

"Will it haunt you? I think you're stronger than that. Plus, it was only a week, hardly the same as when your boyfriend of three years turned out to be a scumbag."

"I know. I'm just not used to dealing with using my magical senses again. It makes it all that much more personal when you can actually feel what they feel."

"He was an over-confident arse who underestimated you. And don't you dare waste a minute thinking of what might have been if he wasn't a murderer, he was about to skip the country without a backward glance."

"I'm not thinking that. I'm far more freaked out by how nice you're being."

"It's temporary," Morwenna reached out and grabbed the last fish-finger out of Morgana's hand and popped it into her own mouth. "Plus, I can afford to be magnanimous, I'm leaving tomorrow."

"So soon?" Morgana failed to hide her grin at this news.

"I got a call this morning, Kelly Ross is in rehab so I can take her part in Othello if I go straight back to London."

"So why haven't you left already?" Morgana teased.

"Curiosity. I want to know the full story before I go." Morwenna took the proffered glass from her mother and sipped it while trying not to grimace.

"I'm sure we all do," Delia agreed, taking the armchair by the window. "Ellie and Gregory will be back soon, but I expect they'll both be very tired and not in the mood for talking."

"Don't ruin the fun part," Morwenna pouted. "I want to hear the gory details of exactly what he was doing in that bar with the dead girl."

"Morwenna Emrys, don't you dare!" her mother reprimanded.

Morgana let her head fall back against the cushions and tuned out their arguing. She knew that Morwenna would ask anyway.

Half an hour later they returned, clinging tightly to

each other. Gregory still looked pale and shaken, but he hugged them all and declared that he just needed a strong cup of tea to be back to his usual self.

"So, go on then," Morwenna pressed Gregory, as soon as he'd gotten his tea, despite her mother giving her black looks. "What's the true story behind what happened that night? Morgana told me about the petrol receipt, which nailed Harry, but nearly did the same to you?"

"You do know I never actually looked at the receipt Harry gave me?" Morgana put in. "It was a total guess."

"No way!" Morwenna actually looked impressed. "Just as well we found your wallet under the car seat on the way here. It's the most important bit of evidence in the case."

Gregory ran a hand through his hair. "I want you all to know that there was *nothing* between myself and Kendra."

"Well, of course not!" Ellie looked outraged that anyone of them would ever think differently, while Morwenna and Morgana exchanged guilty looks.

"She called and said she wanted me to sign a reference for her. I didn't know she'd come into some money and I just thought she was job hunting behind Simon's back. But it was just a ruse." He broke off and blew on his tea looking embarrassed. "She, um, she tried to kiss me and then got extremely upset when I turned her down. She made a bit of a scene, so we left the bar and got into a taxi together because my hotel was only around the corner from her place. I barely spoke to her on the way there, and left immediately when we got out of the cab. But I felt unsettled. She'd come on pretty strong and even though I'd rebuffed her I still felt sort of tainted by it. I just wanted to run back to Ellie's arms and reassure her, or myself, that we were solid."

Ellie, seated beside him, hugged him tightly and he held her close for a long moment, simply breathing her in.

"Go on," Morwenna said impatiently.

"It was stupid really, but I got in my car and began to drive home. I made it all the way to the house before I realised how ridiculous I was being. I couldn't just turn up at 3am and declare to my wife of nine years that I loved only her. I decided that Ellie would think I was drunk, and also, I had an appointment first thing in the morning in Bristol. So, I turned around and went back again. I wish I hadn't now. Nothing matters as much as being here with my family. I'm just sorry you had to go through dealing with a dead body without me."

"You got the worst end of the deal." Ellie's face darkened. "If I ever see that Harry again, I will hex him so badly that he'll be screaming for weeks."

"You are seriously scary sometimes," Morwenna commented with a grin.

"Don't encourage her, revenge is never the answer," Delia said primly.

"It is sometimes."

Morgana closed her eyes and nestled into the couch cushions, just glad that it was all over.

Tomorrow life could go back to normal. Harry was in custody, and Tristan said that Harry's wife would also be facing charges. Her own love life had taken yet another beating, but that was nothing she hadn't handled before. Maybe the next one would be a genuine good guy, or maybe she was fated to always fall for the wrong men? At least she had her cat for company. She briefly wondered if she'd miss having Morwenna around and decided that she wouldn't.

On cue, Morwenna declared, "Well, I'm not sorry to be leaving. Murder aside, Portmage is so very dull!"

Morgana let her tiredness pull her body towards sleep despite the fact she ought to be going back to her own home.

Portmage had a long history. It might no longer play host to famous wizards, legendary kings and Feudal Lords. And there wouldn't be any more epic battles over castles and the beautiful ladies who lived in them. But to call the village dull? No, it would never be that.

There was life in this village, it was a microcosm of the bigger world, and full of interesting people. The castle also remained, which held secrets and ghosts. And there was magic, because Portmage still had a witch or two…

~

Pixie's Place Rhubarb Jam Recipe

Ingredients

- Rhubarb 1kg, washed, trimmed and chopped into 2cm pieces
- Red chillies 4, deseeded and roughly chopped
- Jam sugar 1kg (contains pectin)
- Zest and juice of 1 lemon
- Ginger 50g, peeled and finely grated (optional)

Method

- Step 1

  Put all the ingredients above into a large bowl, cover, and leave at room temperature for 1 hour, stirring a few times throughout.

- Step 2

  Tip into a preserving pan and heat gently, stirring until the sugar dissolves. Bring to the boil and cook for 10-15 minutes until the rhubarb is really tender and the mixture reaches jam setting temperature (105C).

- Step 3

  Take off heat and allow to cool for a few minutes. Pour into sterilised jars and seal.

Tip 1: Put a saucer into the fridge beforehand and when you think the jam is ready spoon a small amount on to the cold saucer. Run your finger through the jam, and if it has reached setting point then it should feel jammy and will wrinkle.

Tip 2: If any foam appears on the top while cooking, don't remove it until the end.

Tip 3: It's best to use a sugar thermometer when making jam so you can check the setting point.

Tip 4: Wait until jam is cold before applying a date label to the jars.

Killer at the Castle

Portmage castle holds many ghosts, but only one of them just died…

When Will Bailey returns to the village to collect his inheritance, less than a day passes before he's murdered. But who'd want him dead?

Morgana Emrys had the misfortune to witness his fall from the ruins of the castle tower to the sea below, and she's far from sure that he was alone up there. Her need to know the truth leads her into an investigation that she might only survive if she can grapple her returning powers into submission before they overwhelm her.

Finding a killer is her first priority, but the ghosts don't want to rest in peace!

Preview of Book Two:

Morgana smiled and waved until the door to her shop closed behind the last of the tourists, then let her expression drop into one of exhaustion.

"Not that I don't appreciate the trade," she told Lancelot, who was stretched out on the counter messing up the gift wrap paper. "But it will be almost a relief when the summer is over and I can tidy up a bit and restock. We're almost completely out of those candles shaped like the castle. They've been a big hit this year."

Lancelot lazily licked her hand as she passed it over

his black furry head, and flicked his ears in acknowledgment. But his expression remained unmoved, which was pretty typical for him. Not much phased the cat, not even flocks of twittering tourists who seemed to arrive by the busload in Portmage during the height of the season.

"I'm starving and it's nearly afternoon tea time," Morgana continued. "I might pop to the café and get a sticky bun of some sort. You want anything?"

Lancelot gave her a disdainful look and she laughed. "Yeah, I know, it's not your cup of tea. I'll feed you at closing, okay? I might even have a bit of fresh mackerel left if you're good. We can fight over it."

Lancelot closed his eyes, so she grabbed her purse and switched the sign on the door. It now said: *Had to fly, back in a short spell,* with a picture of a witch on a broomstick.

Once outside Morgana paused to check the display through the mullioned arches of her shop window. They were definitely starting to look bare since she'd sold that centrepiece wooden fairy castle. She'd been tempted to say it wasn't for sale simply because she loved it so much, and it was unique as it had been hand made by Old Ben, who lived in the woods a mile inland and only just scraped a living from his wood carving business. But it was thoughts of Old Ben that had made her reluctantly agree to the sale. £500 would make his month. Plus she was sure he'd be delighted to know that a little girl had gone into raptures over it, forcing her doting dad to offer higher and higher until Morgana had finally accepted. That was the London lot for you, £500 was probably small change to the child's obviously well heeled father. Anyway, Old Ben might offer to make Morgana another, though she doubted it would be done before the end of the tourist season. It had been a masterpiece, several stories high with steps and towers and little windows and doors, all made of local oak, and it had been a real draw for the eyes of people passing by on their way to visit the real castle.

Morgana gave a shiver as she looked along the cliff to the crumbling ruin that jutted out over the sea, and put her head down against the wind that regularly buffeted the North Cornish coast line, summer and winter alike. She hurried up the High Street and only stopped when she reached the warm and inviting window of the bakery.

Once inside she smiled at the young girl behind the counter and sat herself on a stool by the window. There was a short line of customers, but Morgana didn't need to wait. Lucy had seen her and gave a nod, before calling over her shoulder to the kitchen through the hatch behind her.

"Hey, Ellie. Your sister is here."

A minute later Ellie came out, drying her hands on a tea towel. "Hi Mog."

"Don't call me that," Morgana groused, as she had been doing practically since she could talk. "Were you baking?"

"No, just getting the last of the summer blackberries pulped," Ellie replied. "It should be a good year. The plums look set to be a bumper crop as well, come autumn."

Morgana nodded with approval. As well as a bakery and tea room, Ellie had recently expanded into the premises next door and opened a second business for her extremely popular jams and other preserves. In fact, the new place was called 'We're Jammin'. A name which Morgana had raised her brows at, but Ellie's husband, Greg, had chosen it and he was the money behind the business. All Ellie wanted to do was make jam and bake cakes. Greg was originally from Birmingham and probably equally bemused by Morgana's own shop name, which was called Merlin's Attic as a nod to local history.

Ellie and Morgana were absolutely nothing alike. Ellie had done the traditional Cornish thing; married young, popped out three hearty children, and opened a tea shop. She was also well on her way to being plump and dressed like a motherly matron in chef whites.

Morgana, on the other hand was still very much single, and had embraced her witchy heritage in every way, including her clothes, which were as much for her own fashion sense as they were to delight the tourists. Today's dress was a typical black with silver spider web pattern, that barely disguised more cleavage than was probably decent in a gossipy village. She was also a couple of inches taller than her older sister, and wore her chestnut hair down instead of the bun that Ellie favoured.

Ellie's only nod to her family tree was a sign on the window that said 'Pop in for a brew' and had a picture of a witch stirring a cauldron. She probably only kept it up because Morgana had given it to her.

"Do you have any strawberry jam left? I was hoping for a cream tea to take away." Morgana said, eyeing the shelves where the jars of jam for sale stood, and which looked as depleted as her own shop shelves.

"I would *never* run out of strawberry." Ellie looked aghast at the idea. "We have to be able to do cream tea all year round."

"Oh, okay. Don't people ever eat blackberry jam with their cream tea?" Morgana asked innocently, even though she knew it would get a rise out of Ellie.

"That's not traditional, and well you know it," Ellie said calmly, refusing to take the bait.

"Can't mess with a Cornish Cream Tea." Morgana agreed. "So, can you pack me one up? I left a sign on the door indicating I'd be right back."

"Sure, business is good then? People still want to know their fortune?"

"Not so much, it's more about candles and crystals this year. How about you?"

Ellie gave a happy gesture toward the queue of waiting customers as she wove round the tables back to the kitchen.

Morgana was glad her sister was busy, but it was summer, and summer was always good to them all. It was winter that was bleak. Not just the cold with the wind and the rain, but also the lack of trade. She made a mental note to go to the bank the following morning to squirrel away this weeks takings, before she spent them on the gorgeous new shoes she'd seen while browsing online the night before. The shoes would be wasted in the village anyway. Plus they had heels that she couldn't stand up in all day in the shop. Maybe a new pair of boots instead? She pondered. Nice shoes wouldn't last five minutes before she stepped in dog mess on the cliff path, where people insisted on walking their dogs and never cleaning up after themselves. It was a personal bugbear of hers. But some kick arse leather boots could handle that.

"No no no, save it don't squander it," She admonished herself, unwillingly quoting her late father.

Five minutes later she was back at Merlin's Attic, unlocking the door, when a woman walked past and hissed, "Witch!"

Morgana stopped and stared as the smartly dressed lady stalked on by. That sort of thing hardly ever happened, so it was always a shock when it did.

"New boots it is," she told Lancelot as she went inside. "Some arse kicking may yet be required!"

~

Morgana pondered the brief confrontation as she licked clotted cream off the side of her scone. There had, over the years, been one or two locals who'd objected to her lifestyle choices and had let her know. But it was rare from an out of towner. Especially city folk, they were usually far more worldly, and the woman had definitely been dressed like a city tourist. She'd had an umbrella sticking out of her handbag for a start, and anyone local would know that the coast was far too blowy for such a thing. Also the silly nautical shirt. Only a towny would buy one of those; and white shorts? Rookie mistake in the countryside.

No, usually it was the more elderly types, like Mrs. Gropple, who regularly told Morgana off for being weird, and suggested she should wear some lovely pastels for a change and then she might get a husband. And there was that earnest vicar who'd only lasted one season in the parish, but had made time before he left to come and lecture Morgana on Satan worship until she'd shooed him out the door, clutching his hat in high dudgeon.

It was strange, then, that she looked up at that moment and saw Mr. Bailey go past the window. She remembered him well because he'd been one of those that also made it clear he thought she was wicked. In fact he usually spat on the ground if he passed her in the street. Not that she'd seen him in years. He'd moved away a long time ago, for some reason she couldn't quite remember, even though she was sure it had been a newsworthy story. She'd have to ask Ellie about it next time she saw her.

The bell tinkled over the door, and Morgana quickly shoved her scone under the counter.

"Good afternoon," she said, cheerfully to the young couple who'd entered, before busying herself with a half done crossword that had become smudged with jam. She usually started the crossword when it was quiet first thing, and hardly ever had time to finish it. But it made a good prop, because customers liked to browse and got uncomfortable if you watched them doing it.

"Ooh, this castle is so pretty!" The girl said.

Morgana glanced up, "It's not for sale, I'm afraid, that is, it's sold. But I have the card of the wood carver if you'd be interested in commissioning something." She indicated a stack of cards at the far end of the counter. People hardly ever took one, but pointing them out was the least she could do for Old Ben, especially as he'd made the castle for nothing more than to grace her window. "There's also some lovely oak bowls over there by the same guy."

The bowls were a good seller, and she made a nice commission on those. The wood was gnarly and looked impressively gothic, despite being polished to perfection. They definitely had an artisan quality to them, even though Morgana suspected that most people used them as salad bowls, just as she did herself, rather than for anything more magical.

The girl picked up a small one. "This would be perfect for olives."

Morgana didn't speak this time as the girl's boyfriend was examining the bowls.

"You can get this stuff back home, Kate." He said.

Morgana bit her lip to prevent herself from retorting, "No, you can't."

"Find something a bit more Celtic to remember the holiday," he suggested.

Morgana silently sighed as they went to look at some pewter mugs, which she knew full well were made in a factory in Leeds. She'd just decided they were unlikely to buy anything when the boyfriend sidled over and spoke in a hushed voice. "I want to get the Celtic love knot ring in the window as a promise ring, but I want it to be a surprise. I got this one for the size, I don't suppose you could help?"

Morgana's eyes sparkled. She loved the idea that he'd come to Portmage of all places to propose.

"No problem, settle her in the café down the road, then tell her you need to check on the parking or something, I'll have it ready." Her hands closed over the ring he held just as Kate turned back.

"Colin, look at these tarot cards, aren't they beautiful?"

He frowned slightly. "Tarot cards?"

Morgana decided to step in. "They're not evil or anything, it originated as a card game. Some of these are by a local artist. People often choose their favourite and display it in a frame. Especially the larger versions which you can buy individually. Here, have a look at mine." She plucked her own set from under the counter and spread them face down.

"Choose a card," she told the girl.

The girl gave a giggle and her finger hovered over the backs. "That one," she said, bringing it down to touch a card.

"Nice choice," Morgana commented, then flipped the card. It was The Lovers. The girl blushed and looked at her boyfriend, who gave a rueful grimace.

"I guess we'll be taking the tarot cards."

"We have several designs, would you like me to see which are best suited to you?" Morgana asked.

Kate looked confused but hesitantly nodded, so Morgana reached out her hands and took the girls own. She closed her eyes and tried to get a feel for her vibrations.

She was aware of the bell tinkling again over the door but she didn't open her eyes as she concentrated. Unfortunately, whoever had just come in was radiating angry vibrations and Morgana felt them more than she'd like as she already had her senses open. She grit her teeth against the waves from the newcomer and focused hard on Kate.

The younger girl had a nervous energy about her, but

that was to be expected, it wasn't unusual for her age, plus she was away from home which always unsettled people's energy centre a little, and she was with her boyfriend who was about to propose. Morgana could feel excitement and anticipation and got the feeling that the girl already knew what was coming. That would make sense, seeing as The Lovers card she picked was about partnership. But behind the nervousness, Morgana sensed a sweet disposition and opened her eyes.

"You need Angel cards, not witch cards." She said with a nod, and was convinced she heard a sigh of relief from Colin.

She could still feel the anger rolling off the man who'd just entered, but she ignored him and kept her attention on the couple. She brought out two different packs and the girl made a quick selection, being obviously more drawn to one than the other.

"Lovely, I hope you both have a great stay." Morgana handed over the purchase in a small brown paper bag with the Merlin's Attic logo on the side.

"What we need now is cake." Colin declared, and hustled Kate outside before she could start browsing again.

Morgana watched them go with a smile, then her expression changed as she switched her attention to the man standing in the shadows.

"Can I help you?" She said, not intending her voice to come out as cold as it did.

"Don't speak to me like you don't know exactly how you can help me! A merry dance you've led me, but I've found you now."

He took a threatening step towards her, and Morgana

felt herself take a step backwards, intimidated by his sheer presence.

He was tall, much taller than her own 5ft 8, and though he was dressed in only jeans and a dark blue shirt, his voice was cultured and hummed with fury. His brown hair was tousled and his eyes flashed bright against the darkness of his skin.

"I have no idea what you're talking about." She glared back at him.

"I knew you were a good actress, but pretending not to recognise me isn't going to work." Then he reached out and grabbed her by her upper arms in a vice like grip.

Not knowing what else to do, Morgana released her fear as an energy ball and zapped him.

Get Book Two, Killer at the Castle, on Amazon now!

Printed in Great Britain
by Amazon

77096891R00124